"I once imagined I was in love with Guy."

"Imagined?" Ross's voice was wry. "I saw your face when he was talking to you just now."

"I was happy to see him and Fanny," Emma said defensively. "I'm cured. It was just a brief spell. Nothing real, nothing solid."

Ross watched her, his features sardonic. "And the kiss? What was that for?"

"The kiss?" She looked blank for a moment. "Oh, that didn't mean anything. It was just a brotherly peck."

Ross gave her a dangerous, narrow-eyed stare. "Was it indeed? Well, don't ever confuse me with him, will you. Brotherly pecks aren't in my line."

Emma *was* confused. Her heart thudded. What did he mean...?

Books by Charlotte Lamb

A VIOLATION

HARLEQUIN ROMANCE

HARLEQUIN PRESENTS

These books may be available at your local bookseller.

Don't miss any of our special offers. Write to us at the following address for information on our newest releases.

Harlequin Reader Service
P.O. Box 52040, Phoenix, AZ 85072-2040
Canadian address: P.O. Box 2800, Postal Station A,
5170 Yonge St., Willowdale, Ont. M2N 6J3

Kingfisher Morning

Charlotte Lamb

Harlequin Books

TORONTO • NEW YORK • LONDON
AMSTERDAM • PARIS • SYDNEY • HAMBURG
STOCKHOLM • ATHENS • TOKYO • MILAN

Original hardcover edition published in 1977
by Mills & Boon Limited

ISBN 0-373-02696-X

Harlequin Romance first edition June 1985

CHAPTER ONE

A tear trickled down Emma's cheek. Angrily, she brushed it away and fixed her mind upon the task in hand. She had another twenty miles ahead of her and her sense of self-preservation warned her that it was dangerous to think about Guy and Fanny. She needed to concentrate on the road. The sky was already turning a deep, luxurious purple, the colour of ripe plums. In this strange half-light it was easy to make mistakes. Shadows could play queer tricks. She disliked night driving, anyway, and wanted to reach her destination before night really fell over the curved Dorset landscape.

'Why Dorchester?' Fanny had asked blankly, watching her pack that morning.

'I've been commissioned to illustrate a new American edition of Hardy's books,' Emma said, sticking to the exact truth. The letter of the law, if not the spirit, she thought, blindly packing some clean handkerchiefs.

Fanny had given her a sidelong, anxious look. They had shared a flat for two years. They knew each other as well as it is possible for two girls to do

—they both hated tomato ketchup, both loved cats, both hated opera, both adored liquorice. Where they differed the division was cheerful. Fanny liked watching sport while she sat comfortably at home in front of the television with a box of toffees. Emma preferred to join in, playing squash, badminton and tennis with energy and ferocious enjoyment. Emma liked the windows open. Fanny liked them shut. Since they had had to share a small flat, they had learned to compromise. It was, as Fanny had often said, a good preparation for marriage.

What neither had ever anticipated was that they would fall in love with the same man.

Emma had met him at a tennis tournament one hot June afternoon. There had been silver birches casting a moving shadow at the edge of the courts. Emma had played against Guy in a doubles match, beating him and his languid partner hands down. Over tea and iced buns they had discovered a great deal in common. Guy was tall, fair, energetic. Emma had loved the warm smile in his blue eyes and the little bump in his nose where a rugger ball had made violent contact years ago.

'I went out like a light,' he had grinned. She had been all sympathy, wondering what sort of schoolboy he had been, absurdly touched by the thought of him at such a tender age.

By chance, Fanny had been on a month's trip to America, a long sales tour with her publisher boss. It was three weeks before she met Guy, and by then Emma had fallen in love with him, believing or hoping that Guy felt the same about her.

They were in the flat playing a noisy game of cards when Fanny arrived home. It was raining hard, the wind blowing fiercely against the windows. Fanny stumbled into the flat, shaking the rain off her coat like a small, fussy dog. 'Good lord, what a homecoming! Is it laid on just for me ... English rain! It smells heavenly after a month of Californian sunshine!'

Fanny was tiny, delicate, her head a mass of soft golden curls. Her skin was a glowing peach colour, warmed by golden suns far away. Against it her blue eyes seemed incredibly vivid, especially as she laughed at them.

'Oh, Em, I'm so glad to be home!' Her eyes rested on Guy, mildly curious for an instant, then widening oddly.

Guy had turned dark red and was openly staring. 'You're Fanny ...' he stammered in the tones of one who had just seen Aphrodite rising from the blue waters of the Mediterranean.

Emma had felt a coldness around her heart. She looked from one to the other, at first incredulous, then despairing. She had never seen it happen before, but there was no mistaking what this was—Guy was too direct and open to hide what he felt, and Fanny was obviously as lit up as a Christmas tree, her heart in her wide blue eyes.

The coldness had deepened over the next week. Guy was always at the flat, but now it was to see Fanny.

Fanny had anxiously inquired as to Emma's interest in him, of course. She was far too honest and

7

kind-hearted to steal a boy-friend ruthlessly. In the past they had never been attracted to the same sort of man, and although Emma had met him first, Fanny believed Guy when he assured her that they had been good friends, nothing more. To Emma herself, Fanny said, 'You would tell me to keep my hands off if you felt it that way, wouldn't you, Em?'

Emma had somehow managed a grin. 'You can put money on it!'

'You weren't seriously interested?' Fanny had pressed eagerly.

'Feel free,' Emma had shrugged. No words had ever been so hard to utter, but despite her own hurt Emma had retained enough rock-bottom honesty to recognise that her two dearest friends had had no choice in what had happened. She had seen it hit them at first glance.

'I've never felt like this in my life before,' Fanny had told her, quite unnecessarily, for that was obvious. 'My head's full of bright lights ... rainbows and fireworks ... Em, I wish I could tell you what it's like.' She had giggled. 'He even hates tomato ketchup! Isn't that providential?' Her blue eyes had darted at Emma gleefully, waiting for her response to this old intimate joke of theirs. It had once been their standard test. Did he like tomato ketchup? If he did ... goodbye!

Somehow Emma laughed, but it was wrung from her painfully, and it was at that instant that she decided to go away. She couldn't bear to stay here and be a polite observer at this love affair. Her courage was not up to such a test. She, too, had begun to learn such small, delightful things about Guy. She had found out that he, too, hated tomato ketchup and loved cats. She had been enchanted to hear that he liked to read detective stories in his bath, and hated finding spiders when he turned the taps on in the morning.

How could she stay and hear Fanny going through the same delightful discoveries? It was not their fault. She was not angry with them. They could not help falling in love. Her anger was all reserved for fate—fate, that had dug this pit for her, and gleefully watched her fall headlong into it.

If one could fall into love, though, she told herself fiercely, one could fall out of it, and old proverbs flitted through her mind. Out of sight, out of mind ... many a pebble on the beach ...

She would forget Guy once she was away from him. She would not even have too many memories to take with her—he had been honest when he told Fanny that they had been just good friends. She had loved that friendly warmth in him, misreading it for patient growth of love. A careless arm around her shoulders had seemed like a declaration. How easy it is to deceive ourselves when we wish to believe something!

So she had invented this trip. The commission was real enough, but she had had no real need to make the journey down to Dorset. She could have found the necessary historical details in London museums, as she usually did—sketching costumes, furniture and architecture from old prints and books. However, she had planned no holiday this year, so a few weeks in the country were quite justifiable, and she could do a number of sketches while she was down there. They might come in useful at some time.

It was a stroke of luck that her chosen profession allowed her such freedom. Freelance and fancy free, she told Fanny with a pretence of cheerfulness. She had drifted into doing freelance book illustrations by sheer chance—she had originally intended to work in her uncle's advertising agency, but a commission while she was still at art college had turned her feet into this other path, and they had stayed in it ever since.

She slowed down to read a road sign, then turned off to the left. Only another half an hour, she told herself, and she would be signing in at her hotel. She was beginning to feel hungry. A good sign, she thought, with grim self-mockery. Didn't you lose your appetite when you were in love?

The deep banks on either side of the road hemmed in the sky. A few clouds seemed to be moving in from the north, and she wondered if some bad weather were not on the way.

Suddenly a dog ran out from an open farm gate, right into the road in front of her. Jamming on her brakes, she began to pull up, but her reflexes had not been as fast as they should have been, and the car skidded over to the left a little. She wrenched on the wheel, righting herself, then felt a jolt and heard a violent crashing.

Her head slammed forward against the windscreen. The wheel rammed into her, forcing the air out of her lungs. For a few seconds she did not know what had happened. Then she shook herself clear of confusion, climbed out and ran towards the rear of her car.

Another car had crashed into the back of hers and she saw, at a horrified glance, that their case was far worse than hers.

Their windscreen was shattered. The driver, a young woman, lay forward over the wheel, blood visible on her face. In the back of the car three children were crying, 'Mummy ... Mummy!' The passenger seat was occupied by an older woman, slumped to one side, her forehead covered in blood.

Fortunately, another motorist slowed down at that moment, leaned out and said crisply, 'I'll telephone for an ambulance. Can you cope until they get here?'

She nodded, breathless and shivering. The driver of the wrecked car was beginning to stir. Emma opened the car door and crouched beside her, gently brushing back the hair from her white face. The lids lifted and blue eyes stared at her blankly.

'Don't get upset,' Emma pleaded softly. 'The children are quite unhurt.'

The pale lips shaped the word. 'Children ...' Panic came into the woman's face. She tried to turn her head. 'Children ...'

'They're fine,' Emma reassured her. 'Really.' She looked at them. Two of them were quite young, she saw, but one girl was around seven, and looked intelligently alert. 'Say something to your mother,' Emma whispered to her.

'We're all right, Mummy,' the girl said bravely, her dark hair pushed back by one nervous little hand.

Their mother gave a rough sigh of relief. 'Thank God!' Then she glanced sideways and gave a cry of horror. 'Nanny ... good heavens, she isn't ...?'

Emma said quickly, 'No, no, of course not. I'll take a good look at her, but I think we ought to leave her until the ambulance men arrive.' She went round and bent over the older woman, examining her as well as she could in the bad light. There was a great deal of blood, but she was pretty certain that it was only a surface head wound. Even a small cut bleeds quite a bit, as she said to the other woman.

'Her pulse is quite strong, so she can't be badly hurt,' she added.

'Thank heavens for that!' The driver closed her eyes. A tear trickled down her cheek. 'What a thing to happen tonight ... what rotten bad luck, that car suddenly braking. I couldn't avoid it ... I saw it swerve over the road and I knew I could never stop in time ...'

Emma bit her lip, wincing. She hurried back to the other side of the car and took the driver's hand. 'I'm sorry ... so sorry, but there was a dog ... I had no time to think. It was my fault ...'

The other woman opened her eyes and looked at her, astonished. 'Oh, it was you?'

'Yes,' Emma said guiltily.

'A dog?'

'It ran out into the road right in front of me—I saw it and instinctively slammed on my brakes. The wrong thing to do, I suppose. I caused a much more serious situation by braking, but I had no time to think about what was the best thing to do. I just acted instinctively. I'm sorry.'

The driver smiled wearily, not unkindly. 'I expect I would have done the same.' She tried to sit up again, and winced. 'Oh!' Her hand flew to her chest and she looked at Emma in panic. 'My chest ... ribs ...'

An ambulance came towards them, lights flashing, and stopped a few yards behind. The men came at a run, took in the situation at a glance and politely asked Emma to stand out of the way.

The police were only a moment behind. They took a statement from Emma, but were kind, if a little dry-toned on the subject of dogs. They looked at her car, and pronounced it fit to drive. When she asked if she might follow the ambulance to the hospital, they looked at each other, then nodded.

The children had been permitted to accompany their mother to the hospital. Emma found them sitting in the office of the ward Sister, sipping hot cocoa and nibbling biscuits. The eldest hailed her almost as a long-lost friend. In this unfamiliar setting she was a link with their mother, in a funny sort of way.

'How is she?' Emma asked the Sister discreetly out of the hearing of the children.

'Comfortable enough, considering,' she was told.

'She broke two ribs and has a slight concussion. She was lucky. Her passenger came off worst— three broken ribs and a nasty head wound. They'll both recover quickly, though. In neither case was the damage permanent.'

'Could I see her?' Emma had already explained how she came to be involved, and the ward Sister looked dubiously at her.

'Well, I don't think ...'

'Please, I want to help, and I might set her mind at rest.'

'For one moment, then,' the Sister nodded. She herself led Emma into the small side ward, and stood at the door as Emma went up to the bed. There was a bandage round the pale forehead now, but the blue eyes recognised Emma, and the young woman smiled faintly. 'Hallo, again!'

'You don't mind me coming to see you? I wanted to see if there was any way I could help. The children, for instance ... could I help there? Please, say I can—I feel so guilty.' Emma smiled at her, brown eyes appealing.

'You mustn't feel guilty,' the other woman said weakly. 'But thank you for offering to help, Miss ...?'

'Emma Leigh, and do please call me Emma!'

'Emma ... lovely name,' smiled the other woman. 'I'm Judith Hart.'

The ward Sister, reassured that all was well, slipped out of the room. Judith Hart gestured to a bedside chair. 'Do sit down.'

14

'Thank you,' Emma said. 'Have they notified your husband, by the way?'

'They can't,' Judith Hart said sadly. 'He's in Turkey.'

'Turkey?' Emma's brown eyes opened wide.

'We're archaeologists, Tim and I,' Judith explained. 'Since I started having children, Tim has been careful to take on work only in this country, so we could have the children with us, but now that they're getting older he suggested we both accept to work in Turkey for the summer. My brother has a large cottage down here in Dorset, and Nanny agreed to bring the children down here to stay with him while we were away. Ross, my brother, has a very good housekeeper, so it was perfectly respectable.' Judith grinned. 'Nanny's French, and very concerned about her reputation!'

'And what will happen now?' Emma asked. 'Will your brother's housekeeper take on the children?'

Judith sighed anxiously. 'I doubt it. She isn't too keen on children, apparently. It was only because Nanny would be in charge of them that the arrangement was possible.' She bit her lip. 'I don't know what's going to happen.' Her eyes filled with helpless tears. She brushed a hand over them crossly. 'I'm sorry ... don't take any notice of me. It must be the shock.'

'Let me look after them,' Emma said impulsively.

Judith stared at her, astonished.

Emma laughed at her expression. 'I'm serious. I'm a freelance artist. I've come down here to do some sketches for a job I'm doing ... a book. I could easily stay with the children while you're in hospital. From what the Sister said it won't be long, anyway. You aren't badly hurt. I'm down in Dorset for a few weeks, and I have no arrangements to be upset ... it won't inconvenience me at all.'

'But do you know anything about children?' Judith asked. 'Mine aren't angels, I'm afraid. They can be perfect terrors when they're in the right mood. Do you think you really want to take on such a responsibility?'

'It would make me feel a lot easier,' Emma said frankly. 'I've been feeling terribly guilty since it happened. It would ease my mind.'

'Then there's my brother,' Judith said, with the air of one who means to be absolutely fair. She looked at Emma meaningfully. 'Not to put too fine a point upon it, he's a male chauvinist of the worst sort. He isn't married, and never will be, I suspect, because he has such a high standard, and no mere woman could ever reach it.' She grimaced. 'Ross and I never got on, to be honest. He doesn't understand why I should want to get back to archaeology. He thinks I should stay with the children. He only agreed to take them when Tim talked to him about it.'

Emma squared her slim shoulders and drew a determined breath. 'I shall cope with your brother, don't worry.'

Judith looked at her, torn between hope and misgiving. 'Oh, it would be wonderful ... but I don't know ...'

16

'Is there anyone else who could take the children? Your mother?'

Judith sighed. 'Dead. And I have no aunts or other relatives suitable. Tim has two very ancient aunts in Lincolnshire, but they could never take on three lively kids.' She looked pathetically at Emma. 'To be frank, I've been lying here worrying about the children. I've thought and thought and no one springs to mind.'

'Then it's settled,' Emma said firmly. 'I'll drive the children down to their uncle's cottage and sort it out with him. I'll be glad to do it, truly.'

Judith looked up at her, saw warm brown eyes, like chestnuts shining glossily on an autumn day; hair which matched in shade and was brushed until it gleamed, a creamy skin and oval face, with delicately formed features. She liked what she saw. It gave her comfort. She sensed that her children would be in safe hands. Emma had such a solid, reassuring look about her.

The ward Sister came back, her brow faintly wrinkled in concern. 'We've rung your brother again, Mrs Hart, but there's still no reply. Is there anyone else we could try?'

Judith frowned. 'He must be out on his rounds.'

'Rounds?' repeated the Sister. 'Is he a doctor?'

'A vet,' Judith said.

'Oh, I see. That explains it. Then I'll keep trying.'

'I'll take charge of the children,' said Emma. She and Judith explained what had been decided, and the ward Sister gave Emma a mildly approving smile. Judith was visibly looking better, more cheerful and relaxed, and the Sister was pleased by this change in her patient.

Emma went out to find the children. She wanted them to see their mother before they left. It would reassure them to know that their mother was in good hands, and that she approved of their temporary guardian.

The eldest jumped up as Emma came and asked eagerly, 'How's Mummy?'

'I'm going to take you to see her in a moment,' Emma told her, smiling down and taking her by the hand. 'I'm Emma. What's your name?'

'Tracy,' said the child flatly. She looked round at her little brother who was trying to listen to his own heart with a stethoscope he had found in a box on the desk. 'Robin, stop that! Put it back.'

Robin was small and round and rosy, with bright dark eyes and a mischievous grin. He was, Emma guessed, about four years old, but sturdily built for his age. He was wearing a red sweater and neat blue jeans.

The third child was asleep, leaning against the wall, her cheek curled up against her hand, her thumb in her mouth. Emma felt tenderness well up within her at the softness of that baby cheek, the golden down of the pink skin, the long curled lashes lying on the cheek. 'Who's the sleeping beauty?' she asked Tracy lightly.

'Donna,' Tracy said. 'She's only three and she sleeps a lot.' Her tone was disparaging. Emma bit back a smile.

She bent and gently lifted Donna into her arms,

18

the heavy little head flopping against her shoulder. A warm feeling grew inside Emma. How wonderful it felt to hold this soft little body, to feel the trustful yielding, the weight of the small head against her.

'Shall we go and see Mummy?' she asked Tracy.

'Then what are we going to do?' Tracy had an almost adult way of speaking. Her eyes were intelligent as she studied Emma. 'Will Uncle Ross come to fetch us?'

'I'm going to take you to him,' Emma promised. 'As soon as we've seen your mother.'

Half an hour later she pulled up at a remote crossroad and stared hopefully at the dark countryside. Judith had given her a sketchmap of the route. This was definitely the crossroads marked on the map, so the road to the left must be the one to take. But if it was, where was the village marked on the map? She saw no lights, no houses anywhere? Had she taken a wrong turning at some point on the way?

She drove slowly along the road. In the darkness it was impossible to see a thing. Then, suddenly, from behind a belt of trees she saw the lights of a house. She gave a sigh of relief. At last!

She counted the houses. One, two, three ... then another gap. Just as Judith had warned her. Three cottages close together, then a copse. Two fields lay between the copse and the next little clump of houses. Then she saw the small, whitewashed inn marked on the map. She turned off past the inn and drove up a very narrow, sandy lane, parked on the grass verge outside the final house in the village.

Her heart sank as she saw that there were no lights on in the building. The three children were all asleep now, curled up beneath a tartan rug in the back of the car, like puppies.

Emma left them in peace while she explored. She found the white gate and pushed it open, followed the winding garden path. The scent of roses, night-scented stock, lavender and other unidentifiable flowers came to her nostrils. She groped her way to the front door, knocked loudly, knocked again. No sound disturbed the house within. She lifted the letterbox flap and listened. A deep-throated ticking came from the hall. Nothing more. She groaned. Was there no one in at all?

Suddenly a sound made her jump. She swung round, heart thumping. Tracy materialised out of the darkness, slid her small warm hand into Emma's cold one and smiled up at her.

'I woke up. We're here. Isn't Uncle Ross in?'

'Apparently not,' said Emma, trying to sound cheerful. 'We shall have to break the window to get in, I think.'

'Isn't the key under the flowerpot?' Tracy asked.

Emma stared at her. 'What?'

'Uncle Ross always leaves it there,' Tracy said simply. 'If he and Mrs Climp are out.'

'Mrs Climp?' Emma connected the name with the housekeeper after a moment. 'Which flowerpot, do you know?'

'Of course,' Tracy said scornfully. 'I've stayed here before, haven't I? Last summer. For a week, just me on my own. It was great.' She led the way round to the back of the cottage, bent and turned over the third pot in a little row beside the kitchen door. She straightened triumphantly with a key in her hand.

Emma sighed with relief. She kissed Tracy warmly. 'Good girl!'

Tracy wriggled, embarrassed. 'It fits the kitchen door,' she said.

Emma tried the key and was enchanted when it turned in the lock and the door swung open. Tracy slid past her and switched on the light. Emma blinked, half blinded by the sudden transition from dark to light. The kitchen was compact, modern, scrupulously clean and tidy.

'I'm starving,' Tracy declared, rummaging in the large white refrigerator.

Emma was alarmed. 'Do you think we should? As your uncle is out?'

Tracy stared at her. 'He can't expect us to go to bed starving ... Beefburgers ... great! And spaghetti!'

Emma gulped. 'At this hour? I could boil some eggs. I'm sure Robin and Donna would prefer them.'

Tracy giggled. 'Are you kidding? Robin loves spaghetti.' She tossed back her dark head. 'I'll grill the beefburgers and open the spaghetti while you fetch them from the car.'

Emma stared at her, stunned by this efficiency from one so young. Tracy was carefully arranging the beefburgers on the grill, her face absorbed, her fingers deft. Then she turned and began to open the tin with a wall can-opener. Emma shuddered, turned and went out to get the other two children.

They were still asleep. She wrapped Donna in the rug, lifted her over one shoulder and Robin woke up. 'I can walk,' he said sturdily.

They found Tracy busily arranging knives and forks on the table. A kettle hummed on the stove. Tracy had made toast with an electric toaster and Emma obediently buttered it at Tracy's suggestion. Her sense of humour made her want to laugh, but she firmly folded her lips together. Tracy was so very adult as she gave her orders. It would not do to undermine her sense of dignity.

Robin and Donna vanished briefly upstairs to the bathroom. They returned and took their places at the table. Emma made tea, found cups and milk, and Tracy began to serve the meal, her expression comically complacent.

Emma did not feel she could manage any spaghetti, but to appease Tracy's affronted feelings she had a beefburger and some toast. The children ate heartily and seemed to enjoy their meal. Tracy smirked when Emma congratulated her.

'I like cooking.'

'You like eating, you mean,' said Robin, his mouth full.

Tracy kicked him under the table and he yelped.

'I think you ought to turn in now,' Emma said hastily.

Tracy nodded. 'I know which rooms we were going to have—Uncle Ross said in his letter that I could have the one I had last year, and Donna could share with me. Robin's room is the boxroom and you can have Nanny's room, I suppose.'

Upstairs they found the beds already made up. Hotwater bottles lay on the bedspreads, so Emma went back downstairs to fill them, while Tracy helped Donna get into her pyjamas. When Emma returned she found all three ready for bed.

She bent to kiss the two girls goodnight. Tracy permitted her to kiss her cheek without enthusiasm, but Donna gave her a warm hug. She was a contented, cuddly little creature, eager for affection.

'Do you want me to leave the bedside lamp on?' Emma asked Tracy gently.

Tracy looked scornful again. 'Of course not! I'm not a baby.'

Donna was already half asleep, curled with her thumb in her mouth, her hair over her face.

Robin was right under his bedclothes when Emma went into his room. She hesitated, then went over to the bed. 'Goodnight, Robin,' she said.

His rosy face poked out, a bright round eye surveying her. He grinned silently. She gave him a quick kiss on his button nose, and he burrowed back under the bedclothes at once. She laughed, switched out his lamp and went out.

For a moment she stood on the landing. The children could be heard breathing in the silence— rhythmic, contented breathing, she decided with relief.

She had got them here safely! They were warm and well fed, tucked up in bed. Now that she relaxed she realised how nervous she had been. It had been quite a night.

She went down to the kitchen and began to do the washing up. When the kitchen was once more restored to its original pristine order she made herself a cup of cocoa and sat down with it, yawning. Then she washed up her cup and saucer, looked round the room once more, and turned to go up to bed. She switched out the light at the door and made her way to the stairs, then realised she had left her handbag in her car.

She went out of the kitchen door and walked through the dark garden. The wind stirred the trees behind the house. The night breathed softly, almost menacingly. She shivered. It was a very remote and lonely place.

She began to walk faster, her heart beating hard. A dark shape loomed up in front of her. She swerved aside, giving a stifled cry, but hard hands caught and held her in a steely grip.

'Let me go!'

'Oh, no, you don't . . .' grunted the man.

She kicked at him fiercely, struggling.

'Keep still, damn you, and let me take a look at you,' he commanded.

She felt him shift his grip a little, then a torch shone straight into her face. She blinked, turning aside.

'Who the devil are you?' her captor demanded.

She had already realised who he must be. Once her first panic fear had subsided, her mind worked a little better. This was the male chauvinist brother himself! She gave a little groan. 'I'm in charge of your sister's children,' she said, on a stifled laugh.

'You aren't their French nanny,' he said disbelievingly.

'There's been an accident,' she explained. 'Oh, your sister isn't badly hurt, but the nanny was, and I offered to bring the children here to you.'

'Then you can just take them back again,' he said forcefully. 'My housekeeper has given in her notice and left. I can't possibly have them here now. You'll have to take them back to their mother.'

CHAPTER TWO

'THAT'S out of the question,' she said in dismay, and he shone the torch on her face once more.

'Why is it?' he demanded. She flinched away from the light, feeling her own anger rising inside her. He was all that his sister had warned, and more!

'Please, stop blinding me with your torch! Are we to stand here all night in this cold wind? Can't we go back inside the cottage?'

'Why were you wandering around in the dark, anyway?'

She explained, and he escorted her to her car and waited with barely concealed impatience while she found her handbag in the glove compartment. An owl hooted derisively as they walked back, and Emma jumped, startled.

He gave a brusque bark of laughter. 'Town-bred, aren't you?'

She disdained a reply.

At the back door he carefully removed his muddy wellingtons and placed them on a rubber mat behind the door, ready to be cleaned later. She followed him into the kitchen. He walked quietly in his thick woollen socks. She studied him curiously.

Although he had his back to her she got a clear idea of him from the aggressive width of the shoulders beneath his old tweed jacket, the arrogant tilt of his dark brown head, the thick healthy hair wind tossed but glossy. He was just over six foot tall, slim and spare of build, but muscled; a man who spent his life in physical activity, not a man who liked a sedentary life.

He turned suddenly, the teapot in his hand, and gave her a quick, all-seeing stare which swept from her glossy brown head to her feet. 'Tell me about my sister,' he commanded.

She drew a breath made harsh by mounting anger. Who did he think he was, giving orders left, right and centre? Her voice was clear and undisguisedly scornful. 'Sure you want to hear? I wouldn't want to bore you.'

His grey eyes narrowed menacingly. 'You won't bore me, Miss ...?'

'Leigh,' she said, nervous under that icy gaze. 'Emma Leigh.'

'Well, Miss Emma Leigh, you jump to unwarranted conclusions, let me tell you. From what you said originally I gathered that my sister was not hurt in this crash ...'

'I said she was not *badly* hurt,' Emma emphasised. 'She has two broken ribs and slight concussion. They're keeping her in hospital for the time being. The nanny is there, too, with worse injuries.

There's nobody to look after the children, which is why I offered ...'

'How did you come into it in the first place?' he inquired coolly. 'Are you a friend of my sister?'

She flushed. 'Well, no. I ... I was the other driver.'

His glance assessed her, suddenly sharp with interest. 'The other driver? Expound, if you please.'

'I braked because a dog ran out into the road in front of me, and your sister's car ran into the back of mine.' She flung the words at him hotly, angry because she was embarrassed.

'And so your Good Samaritan act was, in fact, a cover for guilt?' he finished for her drily. 'You have a nerve, giving me those scornful, accusing looks!'

Her cheeks were burning. There was some justice in his remark, after all. 'I admit I offered to look after the children because I felt guilty about having been the unwitting cause of their mother's accident,' she said in a low voice. 'But I hope I would have wanted to help even if I hadn't been involved like that! I would certainly not turn away three children who needed help, especially ...' She broke off, biting her lip.

'Especially if they were your sister's children?' He gave her a hard smile. 'I lead a busy life, Miss Leigh. I'm totally occupied already. Without a housekeeper, how do you suggest I care for the children? They barely know me. The youngest is only three, the eldest only seven. I can't leave them alone in the house at night if I'm called out on an emergency, nor is it practical to take them with me. Before you start building me up as a selfish ogre, try considering the practical difficulties.'

'You could ...' she began, but he cut her off crisply.

'Find another housekeeper? I've been trying all day, to no avail. People don't want to live in isolated places, especially if there are young children to look after.'

'I was going to say you could try me,' she said when he ended.

He did a double-take, his grey eyes filling with incredulity. 'You? You'd be prepared to run this house?' Then his glance narrowed, hardening. 'Oh, no. No, thank you. Out of the question.'

'I'm perfectly capable of looking after the children,' she said indignantly.

'That was not what I meant,' he said.

'Then ...?'

His eyebrows rose. 'Surely you can't be so unsophisticated? This is a quiet, country district. Everyone knows everybody's business. Do you imagine your arrival went unnoticed? Even though it's pitch dark out there the village will be aware that a car has arrived at my house, that there were children and a young woman in it ... they'll believe you're my sister until tomorrow morning, and then the tongues will begin to wag. They'll have us in bed together by tomorrow night, and on the point of marriage before the week's out. They love to gossip, and since they have so little to gossip about they make the most of what they get.'

She was bright pink, flustered and angry. 'How ridiculous!'

He began to laugh, and she glared at him. 'What's so funny?' she demanded.

'Your face,' he said, his own expression totally changed by a fierce amusement.

'I think you would be weak-minded if you allowed village gossip to stop you looking after your sister's children,' she said tartly. 'But as you're so sensitive, I'll take them to a hotel tomorrow. That is, if you can put up with us under your roof for one night? Or will your reputation be ruined by such reckless behaviour?'

He gave her a long, hard look. 'Quite a little shrew, aren't you? Of course you'll stay here tonight. And you will certainly not take the children to a hotel tomorrow. I'll have to try to find someone. What do you do for a living?' he asked, with polite rather than eager curiosity.

'I'm an artist,' she said.

His smile expressed cynical disbelief, and she felt her dislike for him growing.

'I illustrate books and magazines,' she said tartly. 'That's why I'm in Dorset. I'm doing some illustrations for an American edition of Thomas Hardy, and as this is Hardy's part of the world, I came down here to get the feel of the country.'

His eyes dwelt on her hands. 'I noticed what slender fingers you had,' he said.

She was surprised and flushed. He grimaced. 'I'm a vet,' he said, defensively. 'It's my job to be observant.'

Emma got up and began to wash up the china they had used. He yawned, stretching, his whole body visibly weary.

'Leave that until morning. I'm off to bed. Have you found all you need upstairs? Hangers, a hot water bottle?'

'Yes, thank you,' she said politely. She returned the kitchen to its previous state of tidiness before following him upstairs. She disliked coming down in the morning to an untidy kitchen. It began the day on a wrong note.

On the landing she met Ross coming out of Robin's room, smiling to himself. He grinned at her, shamefaced. 'Just checking ...'

'Don't apologise,' she said. 'I'm glad to see you do have some affection for them.'

'Scold!' he said mockingly.

Within minutes of climbing into bed she was asleep.

She was awoken by the arrival of Robin and Donna on her stomach. Giving a suffocating cry, she heaved them off and sat up, gathering them into her arms. Donna came eagerly, Robin with reluctance.

'Tracy's cooking breakfast,' said Robin. 'Get up.'

'Tracy?' She looked in alarm at her alarm clock. It showed the ghastly hour of seven. She had set it for seven-thirty. That had seemed an unearthly hour the night before. At this moment she longed for another hour of sleep. 'What about your uncle?'

'He's gone,' Robin said cheerfully. 'To see a sick cow. He wouldn't take me with him.'

'Up,' said Donna, patting Emma's cheek with her hand.

'You two go down to breakfast. I'll follow.' Emma crawled out of bed and surveyed the morning with a jaundiced eye, then went into the bathroom. She felt much better after she had splashed her face with cold water and cleaned her teeth. Dressed, she surveyed the view from her window, and was very impressed.

The house lay in a leafy hollow below a hilly wood. The garden was entirely surrounded by hedges more than six foot high. Within this irregular boundary lay lawns, apple trees, vegetable garden, flower beds and a couple of casually placed garden seats. The arrangement was informal, flowing. It almost appeared as if the garden had just grown haphazardly, without previous planning—a flower bed here, a tree there—little narrow mossy paths running between them all, winding in and out, round and round. Shrubs and low stone walls made little secret places in and out of which hopped garden birds; sparrows in demure grey and beige, bluetits, bright and darting, robins whose red waistcoats attracted the eye, chaffinch, starling, thrush and blackbird. An enormous marmalade cat sunned itself on a low shed roof, keeping an interested eye on the bird life but without the energy, apparently, to do anything about it.

'Come on!' Tracy yelled up the stairs.

Emma laughed and ran down to join the children. Tracy had cooked porridge, stickily bubbling in a big copper pan. Robin was busily making lakes and islands in his bowl. Donna was looking mutinous.

'She hates porridge,' said Tracy. 'But it's good for her.' She said it with a prim little glance which made Emma grin.

'What you dislike is never good for you,' she said, removing Donna's bowl. 'How about a boiled egg, Donna?'

'Yeth, pleathe.'

'Yes, please,' Tracy reminded her bossily.

Donna ignored her. 'Negg,' she said. 'Nice negg ...'

Tracy sat down sulkily. 'Mummy makes porridge,' she said.

'She doesn't make Donna eat it,' said Robin disinterestedly.

Tracy stuck her tongue out at him. 'My porridge was lovely,' she said. 'Eat it ...' poking him in the ribs.

Emma tasted the porridge with a bright smile. It was rather like wet cement. She smiled at Tracy. 'You're a very good cook, Tracy, for a seven-year-old. Wait until I tell your mummy how helpful you've been.'

'She made us get up,' said Robin. 'Am I getting an egg? This porridge is sticking my teeth together.'

'All right,' Tracy shouted. 'Don't eat it. I don't care!'

When the eggs were ready Emma gave Tracy a thoughtful look. The little girl was valiantly attempting to finish her own large bowl of porridge, but the effort was clearly reflected in her face. A grim expression, gritted teeth, a clenched jaw ...

'Good heavens, you mustn't eat as much porridge as that,' Emma said lightly. 'You won't have room for an egg.' She whisked the half-full bowl away and replaced it by a brown egg in a yellow egg-cup. Tracy gave an involuntary sigh of relief, then pretended hurriedly to be reluctant to make the exchange. She was, Emma saw, a child with whom losing face could spell disaster.

When they had all finished breakfast, Emma sent them out to play in the garden while she washed up. Tracy's offer of help was gently refused. Tactfully, Emma explained, 'I need you to keep an eye on the two little ones.'

Tracy self-importantly nodded and shepherded them out. Robin gave Emma a sidelong, almost adult wink. Emma stifled a giggle. Robin was a very unusual little boy, she thought—oddly clear-headed for a four-year-old. He had a habit of putting his finger on a situation in a few crisp words. She wondered what sort of man he would grow up into.

Later, she joined them, wearing a pleated tartan skirt, light woollen sweater in a pale lemon shade and a pair of sturdy leather walking shoes. 'We'll make a tour of exploration, shall we?' she asked the children.

They shouted with glee and began to run ahead towards the gate. The grass was already littered with windfalls from the mossy apple trees. Robin bent, picked up one of them; a large russet, encrusted with greeny-grey mould on the side which

34

had rested nearest the wet grass, chuckled and flung it haphazardly over the hedge.

Idly, they all watched it disappear. Then, to Emma's horror, an enraged cry arose from behind the hedge. Robin, giving her an alarmed glance, scuttled behind her skirt.

A face appeared over the white gate. Sapphire blue eyes spat furiously at Emma. 'Who threw that?' The eyes skimmed over them all, settled unerringly upon Robin, peeping sheepishly out from the security of Emma's shadow. 'You? It was you, you little ...'

'Hey!' Emma put in sharply before the angry expletive could escape from those scarlet, enamelled lips. 'Hey, not in front of the children, if you please!'

The other girl switched her gaze back to Emma. She was exquisite, Emma noted dispassionately, her pink-and-white complexion assisted by cunning artifice but nonetheless clearly based upon real beauty, her delicately moulded features framed between the smoothly brushed wings of silvery blonde hair. She wore a timelessly elegant suit in palest sand-colour. The blouse beneath it was the same vivid red as her lips. She would have looked superb, had it not been for the splash of mouldy apple juice which lay across the left shoulder of her suit.

'Oh, dear, I am sorry,' Emma lamented. 'If we had known you were there ... it *was* an accident ...'

'My suit is ruined! I shall have to go home and change ... it really is too bad!'

'Of course, I'll pay to have it cleaned,' Emma

assured her. 'And we are really sorry, aren't we, Robin?' looking down at him commandingly, her eyebrows lifted.

'Sorry,' he whispered, clutching her skirt with one tight little fist.

The sapphire blue eyes were studying Emma. 'Who are you, anyway? The nanny, I suppose?'

Emma hesitated. It was too complicated a story to go into again. 'I'm in charge of the children,' she hedged.

'You don't look much like a nanny,' the other girl said coldly. 'Far too decorative.' Her eyes were hard, her mouth unsmiling. 'Don't get any ideas. It won't do you any good. He's impervious. Better women than you have tried and failed, and I warn you, if you queer my pitch, I'll make you sorry!'

Emma was baffled and angered. 'What are you talking about?' she asked.

The other laughed. 'Oh, come off it! You know who he is, and I wouldn't blame you for getting ideas, but take a gypsy's warning and keep your hands off.'

'Who is he?' Emma repeated. 'Do you mean their uncle? He's the local vet, isn't he?'

The other gave a sharp, unamused crack of laughter. 'You're kidding!'

Emma stared at her without replying, completely bewildered.

The other girl's hard blue eyes searched hers, a narrow pencil of light focussed on her. Then, very slowly, the other smiled. It was a strange little smile. Emma did not like it at all.

'Well, well, well!' murmured the other girl ambiguously. There was a pause, then she said softly, 'Least said, soonest mended.'

'Look,' Emma began sharply, 'what are you talking about? I haven't the foggiest idea ...'

'Never mind,' came the reply crisply. 'I must rush back and change. Just remember, in future, look where you're throwing things!'

The girl disappeared, leaving Emma staring after her.

Tracy was standing at the hedge, quietly picking elderberries. 'That's Amanda Craig,' she now said in a flat voice. 'She lives at Queen's Daumaury.'

Emma looked at her interestedly. The name was familiar. The house frequently featured in magazines as a perfect specimen of the English country house, set in a tiny park in which roe deer roamed, with silver pheasants and peacocks wandering along the rose-embowered terraces. It belonged to old Leon Daumaury, the financier, a bitter recluse who disliked publicity yet, necessarily, attracted it by shunning it so fiercely. Was Amanda Craig related to him, or employed by him? Her expensive appearance could indicate either. But what was her interest in their uncle, and what had she meant by her odd remarks about him?

Donna had slid through the gate and was running off along the lane on her short legs, heading for the inviting shade of the wood.

'Come on,' Emma called to the other two children. 'Catch up with Donna!'

On the far side of the cottage, in the shadow of

the wood, Donna was peering over a fence at some donkeys, their great eyes curious as they stared back at her.

'Barnaby and Jessie,' cried Tracy delightedly. 'They belong to Mrs Pat.'

Emma looked back at the cottage as they climbed up the steep side of the wood. It lay below them, the low creamy stone roofed with a thatch a shade deeper. The walls were thick, and bulged here and there, beneath the eaves and windowsills, yet they had a look of enduring strength. The windows were latticed, diamond-leads, twinkling back in the morning sunlight as though the house was pleased to have them beneath its thatch. Roses, pink and plentiful, climbed everywhere around the walls, scenting the morning air.

'It looks like the cottage the Three Bears lived in,' said Emma to Donna.

The little girl chuckled, nodding.

The wood was alive with birdsong. Squirrels raced up and down the trunks of beech trees, at their most active now as autumn approached and they finished laying in their store of foods. Wood pigeons cooed far away. A jay gave a harsh call and flitted past them, making the children cry out with pleasure in his vivid flashing colours, the electric blue and chestnut brown. Emma followed sympathetically in their wake as they ran ahead, kicking up beech mast and oak leaves, collecting shiny chestnuts from the wet grass, gazing at delight at the millions of cobwebs of all shapes and sizes which decorated the gorse bushes, glittering in the sunlight as it filtered through the leaves.

They came down through the wood, emerging on a sandy lane, and wandered along beside the hedge. Robin gazed into the tangled, twiggy depths, pausing to gloat over the ripening blackberries. 'Can I eat them?' he asked.

Emma nodded. 'Yes, you may eat those, but always ask and show me before you eat any other berries. I'm sure Mummy told you that.'

Donna nodded primly. 'Yes, she did.'

Tracy broke into a run as they reached a long garden which ran up to the little whitewashed inn. A woman came out, a large yellow plastic clothes basket under one plump arm, a capacious white apron enveloping her waist, her greying hair tied up behind her in a neat bun, her rosy face twinkling with smiles. 'Mrs Pat!' called Tracy.

'Well, now! If it isn't Tracy ... my word, you've grown! Leggy as a young colt, you be.' She put down her basket, with its snowy white contents, and bent to scoop up Donna, giving her a large warm kiss. 'You're a proper little lovie, aren't you? And that's Robin, is it? My word, you've grown too ... last time I set eyes on you, you were a babby, and now you're a young man.'

'I'm four,' Robin informed her, his smile kind but pitying.

Mrs Pat laughed, winking at Emma. 'Aye, so you are! You remind me of your uncle Ross when he was your age.'

Emma looked at Robin, open-eyed. Yes, she thought to herself, that explained a great deal. So that was how the chicken came out of the egg!

'Come along in and take tea with me,' Mrs Pat invited, smiling. 'I've got the kettle on.' She winked. 'I always have it on!'

The enormous, cosy kitchen faced three sides, airy and bright, with the wood through one window, the open fields on view through another and the garden through a third. A small black kitten slept on the rag rug in front of the stove. A kettle hummed busily on the hob. The children were soon seated round the long deal table, eating with the appetite of youth from a plate piled high with hot, fluffy scones. The butter was pale and cold, the jam home-made.

Mrs Pat gave them cold milk, at their request, but made tea for herself and Emma, in a fat teapot the colour of the shy chestnuts they had found in the wood.

Emma told her how she came to be in charge of the children, and Mrs Pat laughed. 'Ross won't like that.'

'He doesn't,' agreed Emma. 'He wants to find someone to sleep in the house at night ... to chaperone us!'

'I'm sure he does,' nodded Mrs Pat.

'It seems a bit old-fashioned,' Emma said, 'with three children there.'

'Ah, well, sometimes one has to be very careful,' said Mrs Pat. She studied Emma closely. 'Tell me about yourself, m'dear ... come from London, do you? You're a long way from home.'

Emma found herself talking. Mrs Pat skilfully,

tactfully, almost unnoticeably, drew from her every detail of her life and background, listening intently. Emma even found herself confessing to her abortive love affair, to her pain over Guy, her decision to run away and leave him to Fanny.

'In a way, I'm grateful all this happened,' she admitted with a grimace. 'So much has happened in the last twenty-four hours that I've almost forgotten Guy.' Certainly the sharp sting of the pain was less. She could think of him with less grief.

A squawk from the garden attracted the children's notice, and Emma glanced out. A large, white-haired woman stood by a far hedge, scattering food for a flock of small, brown bantam hens which excitedly fought for it, wings flapping, leaping at each other with loud cries.

'My sister Edie,' said Mrs Pat, with a sigh. 'She never married, Edie didn't. A loving, gentle creature, works like a demon, but she was never what you might call bright ... slow thinking, see. I don't see why Edie shouldn't come down and give you a hand while you and the children are at the cottage. She's scared of men, though, so while Ross is around she'll shrink into herself. That's why he never asked her to come. He knows how she is ... But she does love children so! It would please her to be with them.'

Emma watched as the three children raced out to talk to Edie, to help her feed the hens. They saw her look round at the house, alarmed, trembling a little.

'She's afraid Ross is here,' said Mrs Pat, sighing.

Then Tracy talked, and Edie visibly relaxed, bending to let Donna take a handful of hen food to scatter. The grains fell haphazardly, and the hens fought and squawked. Donna laughed out loud. Edie laughed, too. Despite the gap in their age, they looked oddly alike at that instant. Emma was touched.

Edie came shyly into the kitchen later, pink and nervous as she glanced at Emma. Her skin was weathered and innocent of make-up, her blue eyes gentle and wistful. From time to time she looked at Donna, eagerly, with uncertain but touching delight. Once she offered Donna a biscuit, her wrinkled brown hand briefly touching the child's smooth cheek in an infinitely touching gesture.

'They're needing help up at Rook Cottage,' Mrs Pat said quietly. 'I said you might be willing.'

Edie looked uneasily around her, alarmed at the idea.

'Please come and help,' Emma asked softly. She gave Donna a little push. 'The children would like it, wouldn't you, Donna?'

Donna willingly went forward and leant against the old woman's lap, her bright gaze lifted. 'Yeth,' she nodded.

Edie fingered a wisp of Donna's hair, her face aglow with loving tenderness. 'Well, I might ...' she said in her slow Dorset drawl.

They went back to the cottage together. Donna held Edie's hand and talked softly, confidingly, as they walked alone, at Donna's stumping pace. Edie was totally intent, her face happy. Robin had found a forked stick with which he intended, he said, to capture snakes. He practised, meanwhile, with pieces of grass and branches as he passed. Tracy walked with Emma, talking about her father. She clearly missed him very much. Emma gained the impression of a happy, united little family, and worried in case Tracy might be secretly unhappy beneath her bossy exterior.

Ross was in the kitchen, banging cupboards and looking like a thundercloud.

'Where the devil have you been?' he burst out as they entered.

Edie turned white, and Emma looked at her anxiously. 'Take the children upstairs to wash, will you, Edie, please?' she asked her.

Edie hurried to obey. Ross stared after her, his brows black above his imperious nose.

'What's she doing here? By the way, I've fixed up a chaperone ... she'll be here at any moment.' He spoke tersely.

Behind Emma a clear, sweet voice said, 'I'm here, Ross darling.'

Emma knew who it was before she turned and saw the sapphire blue eyes and silvery hair.

Amanda Craig gave her a smile which only touched her mouth. 'I'm going to be your chaperone.'

'Oh, dear,' said Emma, looking back at Ross. 'I've fixed up someone, too, I'm afraid ...'

'Then you can unfix it,' Amanda said tightly. 'What a nerve! Whose house is this? Ross makes his own arrangements. I'll move my things into my room, Ross . . .'

'Edie?' Ross was quick-witted, Emma saw. 'How did you talk Edie into coming here? She's petrified of me.'

'You mean that simpleton from the pub?' Amanda laughed scornfully and shrugged her elegant shoulders. 'Well, really! What use do you think she would be? I'll tell her to go home.'

'No!' said Emma angrily. If anyone was to tell Edie, she would. She had made the arrangement, and she was determined that Edie's feelings should not be hurt. Amanda would undoubtedly do harm. She had a way of saying things which bit deep, and Edie was more sensitive than most. Amanda might harm her deeply.

'No!' Ross agreed firmly. 'I think that arrangement would be much more suitable.'

Amanda went dark red and drew an angry breath. 'Ross! You'd rather have a simple-minded village woman than me? You can't leave her with Judith's children!'

'Mrs Pat might be offended if we made it clear we preferred you to her sister,' Ross said diplomatically. 'And I can't afford to offend Mrs Pat.'

'Oh, don't be ridiculous,' Amanda burst out.

Ross gave her a hard look. He said nothing, but she flushed and bit her lip.

'I was so looking forward to getting to know Judith's children,' Amanda said sweetly, after a moment. 'I thought you agreed that I ought to know them better? And really, Ross—that simple-minded old thing! How could anyone take her seriously as a chaperone?'

'She'll be ideal,' Ross said quietly. 'She loves kids, she'll keep out of my way, and she will be no trouble.'

Amanda gave him a stricken look, and Emma suddenly felt sorry for her. She did not like the girl much, but her own recent love affair had made her ultra-sensitive, and she saw that Amanda was wounded by Ross's implied snub.

The blue eyes darted her a furious, hate-filled look. 'Very well,' Amanda said with dignity. 'If that's your decision, Ross, I'll go.'

'Thanks for offering to help, anyway,' he said casually, his hands on his hips, his back half turned to her as he looked out of the window at the sky. 'It's turning stormy. That sky promises rain. You'd better hurry back.'

Amanda looked at his profile, then back at Emma. She turned on her heel and slammed out.

'You were a bit casual,' Emma said, indignantly, to his averted head.

He turned, raising a black brow. 'What makes it your business?'

'Common humanity,' she flung.

He laughed. 'Long words for a little girl!'

'Oh!' She felt like stamping, but controlled herself. It would only confirm him in his self-conceit.

He surveyed her with mocking amusement. 'It was a brainwave to get Edie, all the same. Thank you. I was very reluctant to give Amanda a foothold in this house. She's an inch-taker.'

'A what?' She looked puzzled.

'Give her an inch, she takes a mile,' he said. 'She's been trying to worm her way in here for months.'

'Why, you conceited ...!' Emma was almost dumb with scornful disgust.

He grinned. 'Oh, I don't lay it at my personal door. I don't labour under the illusion that I'm irresistible!'

She was baffled, and stared at him, frowning. He stared back, his eyes searching her face. A little smile hovered at the corners of his lips. 'Your face is like wellwater,' he said. 'Clear and guileless!'

'Do you imagine that that's a compliment?' she asked, her tone filled with insulted irritation.

'It is to me,' he said. 'I'm sick of masks.'

. His face had a sudden cold, clear anger, that she did not understand, but which worried her. Why did he believe that Amanda wanted to get into his house, if she was not in love with him? And what had Amanda meant by her cryptic remarks earlier? There was something here that Emma did not understand.

CHAPTER THREE

'WHERE are the nearest shops? I need to do some shopping—Tracy needs new hairclips and I need some tights. I gather there's no shop in the village.'

'Mrs Pat sells odd items,' Ross informed her, then gave her a thoughtful look. 'But I imagine you could do with a break. Why not come into Dorchester with me today? I've got surgery at nine. If you can get the children ready by half past eight you can all come. You can have lunch there, make a day of it. It might amuse the children to look round the Dorchester Museum. It specialises in country objects—old tools and cart wheels, horse harness ... that sort of thing.'

'It sounds fascinating,' Emma agreed enthusiastically. 'It would be ideal for me, too. I can do some of my sketching while I'm there.'

'Of course,' he said slowly. 'I forgot—you have a commission to fulfil.' His grey eyes narrowed on her face. 'You must be a pretty good artist to get such a commission.'

She shrugged. 'I was lucky.'

His left eyebrow flipped upwards ironically.

'Modest, too.' His tone was mocking.

'I was being honest,' she said sharply. 'I can't pretend that I'm a great artist. I'm capable, that's all. And I've been lucky all along with these commissions out of the blue. A successful career is often part luck, I suspect. Mere talent isn't enough.'

'You enjoy your work?' he asked, crunching the last of his toast with obvious enjoyment.

'Enormously.' She cleared the table, called the children from the garden, where they were playing some sort of game. 'Get ready to go. We're going into Dorchester with your uncle.'

'I'll help Donna,' said Tracy, seeing Emma's glance resting on her little sister. She seized Donna's resisting hand and marched her off. Donna gave the two adults a comical look of resignation.

'What about marriage?' Ross asked, standing up, his broad shoulders looking broader than ever in a shaggy tweed jacket.

Emma was startled. She lifted wide eyes to his face. 'What? How do you mean?'

'Will you continue working after marriage?' he asked lightly. 'So many women do these days.'

'And you don't approve, I suppose?' Remembering what his sister had said about his autocratic, chauvinistic attitudes Emma was ready to flare. 'Until the children arrive I don't see why a woman shouldn't go on working. Young married couples need all the money they can earn. How else can they buy a house, furnish it, have holidays?'

'You do jump to conclusions, don't you?' he said coolly.

'Your sister said . . .'

'Oh, my sister!' He grimaced. 'Judith and I have always been at odds. You mustn't believe everything she tells you.'

The children galloped towards them. Robin's coat looked lopsided, Emma knelt down to un-button it and re-button it. 'You started with the wrong button, darling,' she told him gently.

'Tracy did it,' Robin said, bored and distasteful. 'I told her, but she wouldn't listen.'

Tracy looked furious. Ross took her hand and smiled down at her with a charm that dazzled and astonished Emma. That charm had never been turned on for *her*, she thought; oddly, foolishly al-most jealous of Tracy's good fortune. 'Some people are never grateful, are they, Tracy?' Ross asked the little girl sympathetically.

Tracy gave Robin a toss of the head, smiled at her uncle, showing a sudden gap enchantingly to the left side of her mouth. 'I lost a tooth last night. See?'

'Did you put it under your pillow for the fairies?' asked Ross soberly.

Tracy looked hesitant.

'Yes, she did,' Robin said clearly. 'And the fairies had better leave ten pence, because things are going up all the time.' His voice imitated Tracy's deter-mined accents, leaving them in no doubt as to the origin of the quotation. Tracy went pink and glared at him.

Ross grinned. 'We'll have to wait and see if the

fairies can afford a rise! It was threepence when I was your age.'

Robin regarded him pityingly. 'Gosh, that must have been ages ago. Were you alive in Queen Victoria's time? Daddy's got a Victorian desk. He lets me sit at it and swing round in his chair.'

Ross gave Emma a sidelong glance, full of wry humour. 'I often feel like a Victorian relic, Robin, but in fact I'm not quite that old.'

In the car the children arranged themselves on the back seat, with some squabbling, while Emma sat in the front beside Ross. He drove fast, but skilfully, taking back roads unhampered by traffic. The lanes were narrow, high-banked, with fields on all sides. Cows grazed peacefully in the green meadows. This was fine pasture land, he told Emma casually. 'The chalk uplands over there afford good grazing for sheep. They even graze them on Maiden Castle.'

'I must see that,' she said eagerly. 'Is it possible to reach it by bus?'

'If I get time I'll run you over there this afternoon,' he offered. 'It will depend on my timetable. I've often spent an afternoon up there, eating a few sandwiches, just lying in the grass and listening to the larks.'

'It's an Iron Age fort, isn't it?'

'Yes, they threw up a succession of earth banks, forming rings, although they're more like ovals than circles. They lived in the middle, and it was hard for an enemy to find his way into the place. They put up gates, of course, in the weak spots, and had men posted on the tops of the banks throwing spears and stones as the enemy tried to storm the bank. Any enemy had to cross the ditch below, and it was an easy matter to chuck a few rocks on to his head. If one bank fell to the enemy, they retreated to the next one, and began again. The centre was the safest place, the sanctuary for the women and children. The banks were like city walls, but there were more of them. It was a good idea.'

'Until the Romans came,' she murmured, shivering a little.

'Yes,' he agreed. 'A superior technology, as always, won the day. The Romans were able to use their ballisters, their catapults, to launch iron-tipped bolts over the ramparts—rather like using modern guns against savages. The Romans didn't need to come within arm length, so the unfortunate British couldn't make much use of their favourite weapon. They couldn't chuck their rocks far enough to reach the Romans until after they'd already been decimated by the Roman barrage. It was like the Germans launching a blitz on London, to soften up enemy resistance, before they planned to invade—and in the case of Maiden Castle, the Romans followed on the heels of their Blitz, and easily took the place.'

'And now it's just a deserted earthworks in the middle of fields,' she said sadly. 'Hardy often mentions it. It made a deep impression on him, I think —seeing that pathetic reminder of the past on the horizon day after day. No wonder he was inclined to be melancholic.'

'Oh, I think he would have been, anyway,' said

Ross firmly. 'It all depends how you look at things. The battle of Maiden Castle was centuries ago. Think how much easier life is for the people around here now! I know I'm glad I didn't live two thousand years ago. Hardy should have gone in for positive thinking.'

'Like you,' said Emma drily.

He gave her a shrewd smile. 'I have no time for pessimists. Life is too short.'

They were approaching Dorchester now, negotiating the bridge over the winding river Frome. 'Grey's Bridge,' said Ross quietly. 'It was built by Lora Grey, heiress of a local family. You see that metal plate fixed to the bridge? It's a modern replica of one put up in George the Fourth's time, threatening anyone who defaces the bridge with transportation for life.'

'Heavens!' Emma stared as they whisked over the bridge. 'They were certainly tough on vandals in the nineteenth century!'

'I shouldn't think they had many with punishments like that,' Ross said. 'I often think I'd like to bring back some of those old punishments when I see the cruelties practised by hooligans. I had to put down a dog yesterday. Some boys had thrown stones at it. I felt like giving them a damned good hiding, I can tell you—if I'd known who they were I think I would have done!' He looked grim, his jaw set and his lips unyielding.

'It makes my blood boil when I read about things like that,' Emma agreed hotly. She shot him a little glance. 'I notice you have only one cat? No other pets?'

He shrugged. 'I had a dog—spaniel. He was two when he was knocked down and killed outside the house. A lout driving a sports car—he didn't even stop, just shot off at seventy miles an hour. At least Lucky didn't suffer. He was killed outright. That was my only consolation.'

They parked in a tiny space outside an old stone building with a mossy, tiled roof.

Ross looked round at the excited children. 'Want to come in and see my surgery before you go off shopping?'

From a gate at the side emerged a young woman in black trousers and a blue fisherman's sweater. 'Well, what have we here?' She peered at the children through the car door, grinning at them. 'Come to visit your uncle, have you? Hello, Tracy. Remember me? Good heavens, you've grown like a beanstalk! You'll make Tommy feel envious. He's only grown one inch this year. Remember you measured yourselves in the kennel yard? You must chalk up a new line for yourself while you're here.' Then, without waiting for Tracy to reply, she turned to smile at Emma. 'Hello, you must be the nanny. I'm Mrs Bellent—Chloe. My husband is Ross's partner.'

'Take a breath, Chloe, for God's sake,' said Ross easily. 'Let me introduce you. This is Miss Emma Leigh. She's looking after the kids, but she isn't a nanny, she's an artist on the Thomas Hardy trail.'

'Oh, not old Hardy,' said Chloe irreverently.

'Doesn't anyone come to Dorchester for any other reason? Come in and have coffee, Emma. I expect you need it. Come on, kids, shake a leg. We'll have. fizz and cookies in the kitchen. Tommy! Tod! Come out, come out, wherever you are ... we have visitors!' Her voice swelled to an organ note, rich and round, almost deafening. Two little boys in identical green denims and sweaters appeared from the yard behind the gate. They looked like miniature versions of their mother, fair and round and friendly.

'Come and have a ride in our wheelbarrow,' they invited at once, and Robin, Donna and Tracy were not slow in accepting the invitation. The five children disappeared from sight, chattering with that easy comradeship which children can attain in a moment, and which adults envy.

'Fizz and cookies on offer!' yelled Chloe after them. There was no reply.

'They'll come when they want it,' she shrugged.

'I'm going in to surgery,' Ross said.

'Come to the kitchen when you're through,' she smiled at him. 'I'll look after Emma for you.'

He shared a wry glance between the two of them. 'I've no doubt you will!'

When he had gone into the front door, Chloe smiled at Emma. 'I don't like the way he said that, do you? There was a sardonic ring to his voice. Are you having trouble with him? He's a bit agin women at present, I know—single women, that is.' She grinned impishly at Emma. 'I'm safe, of course, being Edward's wife. No one could prefer Ross to Edward!'

Emma laughed. 'I'm sure your husband would like to hear that!'

'Oh, Edward knows,' she said with a twinkle.

They walked through into the kitchen. Chloe put the kettle on, fished out a tin of home-made biscuits and laid out cups. 'It will have to be instant coffee. We're on an economy trip.'

'Who isn't?' nodded Emma.

'Too true,' sighed Chloe. 'Now, tell me about yourself, and how you come to be looking after Judith's children ...'

Emma related the story of her adventures, while Chloe made the coffee and listened with great interest. 'Lucky for Ross that you turned out to be able to take care of the children!'

'He didn't want to have me there, though,' said Emma.

'No, well, he wouldn't!' Chloe said reasonably, as though that must be obvious.

'Why not?' asked Emma curiously.

Chloe looked at her, wide-eyed. 'Don't you know? Good lord! Well, in that case, I don't think I'd better tell you.'

Emma felt a wave of sheer temper. 'I'm beginning to feel quite claustrophobic about this! People keep dropping hints, then shutting up ... he isn't Bluebeard, is he?'

Chloe laughed cheerfully. 'Good lord, no. It isn't a disreputable secret! Poor old Ross! What have you been imagining?'

'As no one will tell me anything, imagination is all I have to help me,' Emma pointed out.

The children suddenly boiled into the kitchen, chattering like magpies, and Chloe began serving them mugs of fizzy lemonade and plates of the home-made crunchy cookies. 'Coconut or short-cake,' she told them. 'Take your pick.'

'I had a ride in a wheelbarrow,' Robin told Emma. Donna leant against Emma's knee, not saying anything, but blissfully smiling. There was dirt on her nose and a smudge across her cheek. Her eyes shone like blue stars.

'Leave them here while you do your shopping,' Chloe invited. 'They'll be no trouble. I'm used to having kids around the place all day. You and Ross must have lunch here, too. I've got a casserole in the oven—oxtail and dumplings. There's always plenty and casserole stretches easily. I'll just add a few more dumplings, and then make another apple pasty to follow. Do you like apple pasties, kids?'

They all chorused agreement, and Chloe grinned. 'That's settled, then.'

'You're very kind,' Emma said warmly, liking her more and more.

'Nonsense. I love having people to visit. It makes life so much more interesting.' They chatted while the children consumed their elevenses, then there was a noisy exodus once more, and the two young women washed up in friendly co-operation, returning the kitchen to its former tidiness.

Then Ross arrived, with Edward Bennett, and Emma turned to meet Chloe's husband, only to be taken aback to find herself face to face with the most strikingly handsome man she had ever set eyes on. Chloe giggled at her incredulous expression. Edward, half laughing, half blushing, held out his hand.

'Hello. So you're Emma. Ross has told me all about you.'

Edward was six foot tall, as blond as his wife, with lean, bronzed features of film star good looks. His blue eyes were set between thick dark lashes. His nose, mouth, cheekbones all finely modelled. Emma would not have been surprised to find him as vain as a girl, but he seemed, on the contrary, to be a shy and quiet man, with a gentle smile and soft voice.

It was touching to see the warmth in the look he exchanged with Chloe as he refused a cup of coffee. 'I must dash. Mrs Fry wants me to call and look at her poodle. She thinks it has pneumonia.' He winked. 'I diagnose a slight sniffle. That animal is totally spoiled. What a pity she never had children.'

'For whom?' Ross asked wryly. 'Just think what terrible lives the poor things would have led, wrapped in cotton wool! The woman's a fool.'

'She's probably lonely and longing for affection,' Emma said hotly. 'Women need something to love.'

His grey eyes mocked her. 'Do they?'

Edward kissed his wife and left. Ross sighed. 'I must go, too. I've some house calls.'

'You're eating lunch here,' Chloe informed him. 'It's all settled.'

'I see,' said Ross. 'The freemasonry of women again, eh? Thanks, Chloe. I'm grateful.' He smiled at her. 'Edward's given me the afternoon off. I've promised to take Emma to see Maiden Castle.'

'I'll keep the three kids here while you do,' Chloe promised. 'No need to rush back. Drive Emma around to get a good look at the countryside.' She smiled at Emma. 'We're very proud of our landscape, you know. Finest countryside in England.'

'Why not?' Ross shrugged. He left by the kitchen door, while Chloe and Emma went into the surgery to see the animals being kept in overnight. Some were asleep, awaiting surgery or recovering. Some were eager for attention, particularly a small black Labrador puppy, his paws imploringly raised at the cage door. Emma cooed over him, enchanted by his soft paws and sleek coat. 'I wonder what's wrong with him? He looks fine.'

A cat lay supine on an old cushion, breathing lightly. Chloe glanced at her. 'She's just had an operation—see the stitching. It's amazing how animals recover. Tomorrow she'll be moving about, a bit stiffly, but almost back to normal. Humans are far more hard to look after.'

'Yet animals make me feel so much more moved,' said Emma. 'They're so helpless, so bewildered. They just don't understand pain, or why it's happening to them—and you can't talk to them, reassure them, as you can with people. If only animals could talk!'

'You wouldn't say that if you'd ever had a parrot,' said Chloe grimly. She opened a door and at once a raucous voice assailed them. 'Hallo, sweetheart! Crack a nut, crack a nut ...'

Emma giggled. A vivid scarlet, green and white parrot was scuffling up and down, head bent, round eyes slyly regarding them, from his perch in the corner of the room. 'Is he yours?' she asked.

'He belonged to my uncle,' Chloe said with a grimace. 'When Uncle Bill died he left Crackers to me in his will. I felt I had to take the old scoundrel, but he's a perfect nuisance! His language is appalling at times. Of course, the boys adore him. They would! And I'm always afraid they'll come out with similar expressions in front of clients and shock people for miles around!'

She offered the parrot a nut. He sidled up, snatched it with one claw and bent to inspect it, saying, 'Cor ... lovely! Crack a nut, crack a nut ...'

The children arrived in time to see him eat his nut, and crowded round him, admiring, enthusiastic, while Crackers went through some of his repertoire. Emma quite saw what Chloe meant. As the language became rather more colourful, she whisked the children away and gave them orders to play quietly in the yard with Tommy and Tod while she went shopping. Tracy at once begged to come, too.

'If you like,' Emma agreed. While Donna and Robin settled down to play hide and seek she set off around the little market town to seek various items. She found it fascinating to see how much of the old town was left. Anyone who had read Hardy's novels must recognise certain streets, buildings, names. With delight she walked up Corn Hill and stared at the bow windows of the Antelope, an old coaching inn which figured in several of the books under another name; then wandered up to St Peter's Church, another famous landmark in the town.

Tracy was far more interested in the shops. She had some money to spend, and it was burning a hole in her pocket.

'I think I'll buy a book,' she announced.

They went into a bookshop and Tracy carefully selected a volume of children's stories. Emma added a Beatrix Potter for Robin and a little picture book for Donna.

'Robin likes books about cars,' Tracy said scornfully.

'I expect he'll like the Tale of the Fierce Bad Rabbit,' Emma said quietly.

On their way back, they stopped to take a brief look inside the Museum, admiring the reproduction of Hardy's study, the various pieces of nineteenth-century furniture, the agricultural implements and the fine display of Roman remains which had all been dug up around the town. Tracy grew tired after ten minutes, fidgeting to and fro, her attention wandering. Emma smiled at her.

'Shall we go?'

Tracy eagerly agreed. They found that Ross and Edward Bennett had both returned from their visiting, and were awaiting lunch eagerly. The fragrant odour of the oxtail casserole wafted out to them. Chloe grinned. 'Wash your hands and I'll serve lunch! I think everyone's worked up an appetite.'

The meat was tender, falling off the bone in velvety flakes, and the rich gravy had a delicious flavour. Chloe's dumplings were so light that Emma wondered what she had used to make them ... they melted in the mouth, and were rapidly polished off by the hungry horde around the table. Despite mounds of mashed potato creamed with butter, new carrots caramelised and decorated with parsley, and nutty brussels sprouts, the meal only just managed to stretch adequately. Everyone was ready for the apple pasties. They were made with flaky pastry, the apples golden with brown sugar and dotted with currants.

'Mm ...' said Robin ecstatically. 'I do like you, Auntie Chloe.' His reverent tone made everyone laugh. Chloe grinned at him.

'Thank you, Robin,' she said, in a man-to-man tone. 'I like you, too. I like boys who eat heartily.'

'Does that include me?' asked Ross, tongue in cheek.

Chloe gave him a stern glance. 'Oh, you're a pig,' she told him, watching as he scraped his plate clean. 'And you can make the coffee, which will teach you not to make such a pig of yourself!'

'I shan't want to move after that meal,' he moaned. 'I don't know how I'm to summon the energy to climb up Maiden Castle this afternoon.'

'Maiden Castle?' Edward looked up from his silent contemplation of his empty plate. 'Are you going that way? Could you just drop in at Hook

End Farm and see Joe Wing's horse? It's gone lame again.'

Ross groaned. 'I thought it was too good to be true. O.K.'

They had coffee, at leisure, while the children vanished again and then Ross drove Emma out along the Weymouth Road, past the dark and gloomy shape of Maumbury Ring.

'What's that?' asked Emma, viewing it with alarm.

'I'm not sure what it was meant to be, but it's said to be a Stone Age circle—heaven knows what function it was meant to fulfil. The Romans used it later as a theatre, they lined it with seats. The banks are made of chalk under all that grass.'

They travelled on across open countryside, and even from that distance could see Maiden Castle clearly, the great green ramparts some sixty foot high in places, running for miles.

'Just think,' said Emma, 'when it was first built it must have been even higher. After two thousand years the weather must have eroded it enormously!'

'That's true,' said Ross in surprise, looking at her with a curiously arrested look. 'I hadn't thought of that.'

They drove along a bumpy, chalky track between farm fences and found a rough car park at the end of it. A stile marked the beginning of the track up to the Castle. There were already several hardy visitors making their way along the ramparts above.

It was a steep climb upwards, but the wind rushed over the grassy rings with a freshness which was invigorating, and it was pleasant to stride out, filling the lungs and exercising the body. Overhead hung larks, small black marks against the sky. The sheep grazed quietly around them, tearing at the grass with concentrated intensity.

When they had penetrated the inner rings they walked along the ramparts, gazing down over the countryside with interest. It lay open to their gaze towards Dorchester, the outline of the small town discernible as it was not when one was within it.

'What a superb view,' said Emma. 'It puts one into touch with the past, walking up here.'

Ross nodded. 'Yes, a haunted place, despite its beauty.'

'I wouldn't like to spend a night here,' said Emma, shuddering. 'I can imagine the ghostly voices crying over these ramparts.'

Ross laughed, giving her an indulgent look. 'The wind, my dear girl. I wasn't speaking literally when I said it was haunted. I just meant that it reminded one of things best forgotten ... old tragedies, old griefs.'

Obstinately, Emma said, 'All the same, you wouldn't get me to come up here at night. Although there are no buildings, it has a far more ghostly atmosphere than the Tower of London or Dover Castle.'

'How you women love mystery,' Ross teased. He glanced at his watch. 'Sorry to rush you, but I'm afraid we must go if I'm to take a look at Joe Wing's horse.'

They climbed down and drove on until they

reached a farm track. At the end of it stood a square, no-nonsense house with barley sugar chimneys and a gabled roof. 'An odd mixture,' Ross told her as they got out of the car. 'Joe rebuilt the house after the war, but he used a lot of the old house, so the fabric of the building is partly very old, partly very new. The chimneys are Elizabethan, so are the tiles. Some of the bricks are old, some are new.'

They went round to the outbuildings at the side of the house, backing on to a cobbled yard, and found a gnarled old man forking hay and clover into the feeding troughs in the stables. He looked round, saluted them silently.

'Let's take a look at this horse,' said Ross.

'Aye,' said Joe Wing. He jerked a thumb at the end loosebox. A tall raw-boned bay was standing there gazing at them with a melancholy look.

Ross went in to examine him, and the bay leant idly against him as Ross lifted his foreleg. 'Get off me, you great oaf,' Ross said easily.

Joe Wing chuckled. 'Aye, he's the lazy one, big lummox!'

Ross probed gently. 'I'm afraid he's got a mild strain again. He's always had that tendency, hasn't he?'

'Always been lazy,' said Joe, spitting to one side in contempt.

Ross laughed. 'Oh, I don't think he does it deliberately.'

'Oh, aye, for spite, pure spite,' Joe Wing nodded.

Emma wandered off to look idly around the yard, and saw a cat writhing about in a dark corner of an old barn, her head assaulted by her paws from time to time, her whole motion that of great pain.

She called Ross, urgently, and pointed out the cat. Ross quietly crept up and lifted it, spitting and writhing.

'Wild as a crocodile, that one,' said Joe. 'Farm cats! They never come indoors, winter or summer.'

Ross deftly examined the small creature. It was fine-boned, rough-coated, a thin little creature. With difficulty he opened its jaw and Emma exclaimed in horror as she saw the fish hook caught in its gums.

'I thought so,' said Ross. 'She's been fishing, but it was she who got hooked.'

'She gets down to the stream where the anglers sit,' Joe nodded. 'It isn't the first time one of my cats has come home with a hook in its mouth ... they think they're so clever, nipping off with a hooked fish.'

Ross deftly extracted the hook. The cat spagged him viciously, her lips drawn back in pain and rage, then with an eel-like movement escaped and vanished into the darkness of the barn once more.

'She'll heal in God's own good time,' Ross shrugged. He returned to the horse and Emma wandered back to the car. Ross joined her later and drove her back to Dorchester to pick up the children.

'Stay to tea,' invited Chloe hospitably.

'Thank you, but Edie will be waiting for us,' Emma smiled. 'You've been so kind already. Thank you for everything you've done. I've thoroughly enjoyed my day.'

'Come again soon,' Chloe pressed as they drove away.

'Oh, do let's,' Tracy said eagerly, and the others nodded.

As they neared the village they passed a high-walled park which attracted Emma's attention. Through the open iron gates she saw rolling lawns, oak trees, an avenue of beech trees. She was about to ask Ross about it when she saw the house through the trees, and recognised Queen's Daumaury, unmistakably lovely in the late afternoon light, even in such a flashing glimpse.

Negotiating the narrow bend beyond it, over a low hump-backed bridge, they had to draw into the edge of the road in order to let another car pass over the bridge and then pass them going towards Queen's Daumaury. The car was long, sleek, shining, a powerful, expensive toy. A chauffeur was at the wheel. In the back sat an old man, and beside him sat a familiar blonde head.

Amanda leaned forward to wave to Ross. He gave her a curt nod. The old man glanced at them, then away, without a sign of interest. That, thought Emma, must be the mysterious Leon Daumaury. For such a very rich, powerful man he was disappointingly shrunken, his head averted indifferently.

'Who's that?' Robin asked curiously, in his shrill treble.

Tracy answered flatly without waiting for Ross to speak. 'It's Grandfather, silly.'

CHAPTER FOUR

ASTONISHED, Emma looked at Ross with eyes full of incredulous inquiry, but he was staring straight ahead at the road, and did not appear to have heard.

Their car moved forward smoothly at that moment, and she had no time to ask what Tracy had meant. Robin had said something which Emma could not quite catch, then his voice broke off as Donna, full of wonder, cried, 'Look!'

Her small finger pointed skywards. They all gazed up and a satisfied silence filled the car as they saw a creamy barn owl swoop out of the gabled end of an old barn. Twilight was hastening on; the sky was a dusky grey, threaded with palest pink, and the birds were making their sleepy farewells.

'Hoot, hoot ...' crooned Donna.

'Owls eat mice but not their feet or their tails,' Robin declared calmly.

'No,' Ross agreed. 'The owl wraps up all the bits he doesn't want and deposits them as a pellet.'

'Good idea,' Robin nodded. 'I wish I could do that.' He gazed sideways at Tracy. 'When I had sticky porridge to eat ...'

She went red and glared at him. 'Don't start that again!'

'We're almost home,' Emma said hastily. 'I wonder what Edie has got for our supper? She said something about baked potatoes in their jackets.'

'Mmmm ...' Robin swayed, ecstatic, his eyes half shut.

'And tomato soup,' Tracy added importantly.

'Thoup ...' Donna nodded. 'For me.'

'For all of us, silly,' Tracy told her squashingly.

'Ethpecially for me,' Donna insisted.

The car turned in at the track leading to Rook Cottage. The children abandoned their squabble and craned forward until Robin's sharp eyes caught the yellow gleam of light from the windows.

'We're home, we're home!' shouted Tracy, dancing up the path with the other two struggling to keep up in the rear.

Edie appeared in the doorway, beaming. 'So you are, m'dears. Come you in and have your supper.'

Emma took them up to wash and brush their hair, and when they returned to the kitchen they found Edie contentedly serving hot tomato soup, a swirl of cream emphasising the colour.

'There's a grand fire,' said Edie. 'Why don't you have your supper beside it? I've wheeled the table over in that corner.'

They took their seats round the table, the firelight cosy and reassuring. Rain splattered against the windowpanes. The wind tore at the trees and rattled the brass knocker on the door. Outside the world appeared to be in turmoil. Here, within, they were safe, sheltered, warm.

Ross came down five minutes later, in a mushroom-coloured sweater and cream slacks, his face glowing, his hair freshly brushed, to find them all in a blissful state of content. He stood in the doorway, watching them. The children were drinking their soup, their big eyes alternately fixed upon the bacon and egg flan in the centre of the table and the flickering firelight. Emma had washed her face, too, and had not bothered to put on make-up. Her skin, innocent of covering, glowed like one of those childish faces. Her brown eyes were dreamy.

She glanced round as Ross moved forward. A smile involuntarily lit her face, but it received no return from him. His face was oddly stern, and at her smile it hardened, the brows jerking together.

What was wrong? she asked herself. Why did he look so angry? Had something happened?

Quietly, she said, 'Come and drink your soup before it gets cold.'

He took his seat and lifted his spoon to his lips. Tracy handed him the bread basket and he smiled, taking a piece of bread.

'Edie made it,' Tracy informed him.

He tasted it, exclaimed upon its superior texture and taste, and the children all looked satisfied. Edie was already one of their favourite people.

When they had all feasted upon baked potatoes in their jackets, sliced open and festooned with melting butter; bacon and egg flan and cheese straws, banana fritters and little crisp pinwheel biscuits, Emma took the three children off to bed. Edie begged the favour of actually overseeing their bath and bedtime story. Emma smiled at her, nodded. 'Not a frighty one,' Donna whispered. Edie shook her head, as solemn as the child.

Emma went back downstairs to find Ross just clearing the table. Silently, she helped. They washed up together. Then Edie came down, shyly put the china and cutlery away, ducking her head away whenever Ross looked at her.

They settled down around the fire. Emma was carefully darning one of Robin's sweaters. Ross was filling in a sheaf of official forms, his brow wreathed in frowns.

Edie slipped into the room, whispered that she was 'off to bed' and vanished again before they could do more than say goodnight.

'I wonder if she'll ever get used to me,' said Ross, his forehead clearing briefly, and a spark of amusement showing in his eyes.

The telephone rang. Emma, on her way to the kitchen to find a pair of Donna's slacks to mend, answered it instinctively, Ross actually already rising from his chair.

She recognised the voice at once, her hackles rising at the drawling insolence. 'I want Ross.'

Wordlessly, Emma held out the receiver. Ross took it, his narrowed glance on her face. Emma left the room. She found Donna's slacks, examined the hole over the knee, looked at the scanty turn-up, and realised that she would have to use a contrasting patch. Fortunately she had an old pair of denims in her own case. She managed to cut two circular pieces from the flared bottoms of her own jeans, and sat in the kitchen to patch Donna's slacks so that each knee showed an identical little patch. Donna's slacks were pink, Emma's jeans had been blue, but the colour contrast was not unpleasant.

She heard Ross go upstairs, then heard him coming down fast. He appeared in the doorway, shrugging into his bulky tweed jacket, slipping a mackintosh over the top of that. 'I have to go out,' he said tersely.

Emma looked up, nodded without comment. He had that expression again, hard and sardonic. She felt his eyes condemn her, and wondered what crime she had committed now. What urgent summons had Amanda Craig issued to him? Was he needed in his professional capacity? Or in a more personal sense?

Half an hour later she herself went to bed, having banked up the fire behind its close-meshed guard. She looked in on the children, found them sleeping peacefully. Edie popped her head out of her little room, whispered goodnight once more and vanished. Emma smiled, went into the bathroom and had a slow, cosy bath, then went to bed. She could not sleep, however, so she sat up and did some preliminary sketches for her commission, from memory mostly, but supplemented by some postcards she had bought in Dorchester. Next time she went into the town she must do some serious work, she told herself.

She finally slid into sleep an hour later, but it

was three hours after that she heard Ross come up the stairs. He stumbled over the top stair, cursing softly under his breath. Surely, she thought, he had not been drinking? She looked at her bedside clock, yawning. Two o'clock in the morning? Where on earth had he been until this hour? Amanda Craig certainly had some powers of persuasion!

It isn't my business, Emma told herself, settling back on her pillow. Let him stay out all night! He's the one losing sleep, not me.

Next morning, though, her feelings erupted. She had taken the children for a long walk through the wood, gathering blackberries, had made pastry and peeled apples; made blackberry and apple pie for lunch. Edie had spent the morning down at the inn, helping her sister. Ross had been working, but popped in unexpectedly for lunch as he was out that way.

Emma, just dishing up lamb chops and fresh mint sauce, gave a groan as he appeared in the doorway. 'Why didn't you say you were going to come in for lunch? I've only chops enough for four of us.' She threw a desperate eye at the larder. 'Would sausages satisfy you?'

'I can go on into Dorchester for lunch,' he said brusquely, turning on his heel.

'Don't be absurd,' she snapped. 'Now you're here, you'll eat lunch with us, of course, but it would be polite of you to give me warning in future. I hate to be caught like Mother Hubbard with nothing to offer.'

She rapidly fried some sausages, served them to

him while the others had their chops, with creamed potatoes and carrots and peas. The pie came out of the oven to cries of delight. Ross gleefully accepted a plateful. 'I love free food,' he said. 'It would be a crime to waste hedgerows full of blackberries. One morning we'll go gathering mushrooms, kids, and I'll teach you which you can eat and which you can't.'

The children went out to play in the garden while Emma washed up. Ross lounged in the doorway, watching her, yawning. 'I'm tired.'

'Is that surprising?' she asked sarcastically.

'What's that supposed to mean?' He raised a brow inquiringly at her.

'If you will stay out with your girl-friend all night,' Emma said, then wished she had held her tongue. Oh, she thought—my tactless tongue! When will I learn?

There was a little silence. Silkily, he asked, 'What makes you think that? You were in bed when I got back.'

'If you fall up the stairs you must expect people to wake up,' she said tartly.

'Look, Miss Leigh,' he said very softly, 'you're here to look after the children, not put a twenty-four-hour watch on me. What hour I leave, what hour I return, is my business, and nobody else's. Understood?'

'Perfectly,' she said, her colour high.

'Good,' he returned, leaving fast. Emma heard him drive away, paused, her hands still wet, automatically wiped them on her apron and wanted to scream. He had made her feel like a prying prig, and the worst of it was that he was quite right ... it wasn't her business what he did. Why had she said anything? Would she never learn to be discreet, to hold her tongue?

Later, she walked down to have tea with Mrs Pat, an invitation conveyed by Edie shyly but eagerly. The children, dressed in their best clothes, scampered ahead like joyful puppies, while Edie and Emma came more sedately behind them.

Outside the inn they were passed by the familiar, sleek shape of Leon Daumaury's car. The children stood, mouths open, staring. Edie made a gulping sound, like a fish out of water, her expressive countenance filled with horror and dismay. Emma frowned, wondering what to do, seeing the car slow and then stop. The old man in the back of the car sat, his withered hands folded on the gold knob of an ebony stick, staring at the three children.

Emma, joining them, laid a protective, bewildered hand upon Tracy's shoulders, sensing that of the three children she was the one most disturbed by this encounter. Remembering Tracy's voice when she saw the old man yesterday, Emma was prepared for anything. Could it be true that this was their grandfather? It would explain Amanda Craig's interest in Ross. Presumably, the absent archaeologist father was Leon Daumaury's son. Yet Judith had said that her husband had no living relatives, hadn't she? Had she lied, or merely preferred to forget? A man as wealthy as Leon Daumaury might feel bitter enmity towards a son who married in the teeth of his opposition, and Emma suspected, looking at the icy pride of the old man's face, that this was a man who would certainly oppose his son if he wished to marry someone as cheerfully unpretentious as Judith.

Tracy was glaring at the old man, her small face obstinately set.

Suddenly Emma saw, in a flash of insight, a curious resemblance between them—something about the shape of the eyes, the set of the unyielding jaw, the line of mouth and nose. It was indistinct yet unmistakable.

A bubble of laughter arose in her chest. It was funny, really funny, to see the child and the old man confronting one another in that same fashion. Over sixty years lay between them, yet they had so much in common.

Robin, his head tilted to one side, asked in his calm, adult voice, 'Is that really my grandfather, Emma?'

As if terrified, or angered, the old man leant forward and without a word rapped on the chauffeur's back with his stick. The car purred away. The old man did not look back.

Emma looked down at Robin, then at Tracy. 'You must ask your uncle that, Robin.'

'Uncle Ross never talks about it,' Tracy said flatly.

'Why not?' demanded Robin.

'Because,' Tracy said, her voice uncertain.

'Because what?'

'Just because,' said Tracy obstinately.

Mrs Pat came out, her expression so carefully void that Emma was at once certain that she had been watching from a distance. 'There you are,' she cried cheerfully. 'Come along in and try my coffee cake, m'dear. I've made marble cake for the little ones.'

'Marble cake?' repeated Robin. 'What's that?'

'Ah, you'll like that,' said Mrs Pat, leading him by the hand. She winked at Emma over her shoulder. 'All the colours of the rainbow, that is.'

She was not exaggerating. The cake stood in the centre of the tea-table, in pride of place, covered with thick pink icing sprinkled with chocolate drops. When it was finally cut, it proved to be multi-coloured—streaked with green, pink, chocolate. Donna was enchanted. Robin was downright greedy. Even Tracy looked at it with eagerness.

Emma sat over yet another cup of tea, later, with Mrs Pat, watching the children playing in the garden, feeding the hens and skipping happily around the flower beds. She longed to ask Mrs Pat for the truth about Leon Daumaury's relationship to the children, yet she already knew enough of these quiet people to sense that any such personal question could only meet with a stone wall, They would resent her curiosity, and in any case, refuse to satisfy it. Had Ross and Judith wanted her to know about Leon Daumaury they would have told her all about it themselves. Ross had had the opportunity yesterday. He had not taken it, and that, in itself, told her a great deal. Plainly, he wished her to remain in ignorance of the facts. It was a family matter, and she was not one of the family. She could understand that.

It was Edie who first noticed Donna's absence. Emma heard a little explosion of noise outside, glanced out and saw the two children and Edie staring from side to side. Two children? She jumped up, running out instinctively. Their voices called, 'Donna ... Donna, where are you?'

Emma joined them. Tracy burst out, 'We were playing hide and seek ... Donna hid and we can't find her!'

Edie was panic-stricken. 'I shouldn't have let them ... I never should have let her go off on her own, a mite like that.' Anxiety made her quite articulate.

'She can't have gone far,' soothed Emma. 'We'll spread out, keep calling her.'

Would Donna, triumphant at having escaped finding so far, keep quiet in whatever hiding-place she found? She was so small that it would be hard to see her if she kept still.

They spread out, calling. Down the lane, calling at the other houses, going back as far as Rook Cottage, even penetrating the wood and searching it sketchily, without real hope of finding her there. Edie became progressively more alarmed, more tearful. Even Tracy was now worried. Emma began to wonder, secretly, if she ought not to ring Ross and get a more organised search party out, for it would soon be dark, and Donna was so small.

Then she saw her, in the centre of a field, unaware of anything but pleasure, picking dandelion clocks and blowing them to the four winds, chanting incomprehensibly to herself as she did so.

Relief swamped Emma. She shut her eyes, breathing a prayer of gratitude. When she opened them, relief turned to frozen terror as she saw something else—something she had not noticed at first, absorbed only in the sight of Donna unharmed.

On the other side of the field, his back to the playing child, stood a massive, barrel-ribbed bull, head lowered, staring across the fields towards the wood.

Emma bit her lip, thinking fast. She dared not call out to Donna. Any sound would certainly arouse the bull's attention, the last thing she wanted to do. She must go to get Donna herself, as softly as she could. She advanced to the gate. How had Donna got into the field? Slid through the bars? Or had she, too, climbed over?

Carefully, Emma negotiated the five-barred gate and began walking slowly and silently through the grass towards Donna.

She was almost at Donna's side when the child looked up. A cry of welcome rose to the child's lips, but Emma shook her head fiercely, her finger to her lips in silent warning. Donna's face lit up. She giggled. No doubt she thought it was an extension of the game she had been playing with Tracy and Robin. Emma picked her up, turned and began to tiptoe away towards the gate.

The malevolence of Fate struck a moment later,

while she and Donna were still a long way from safety.

Two crows flew over, quarrelling. One gave a loud shriek of rage and defiance, and Donna laughed.

Emma gave a look of agony over her shoulder, and saw the bull slowly turn, saw the little red-rimmed eyes flare with incredulous offence as it took them in, the nostrils flare and steam, the great head lower.

She began to run, hampered by Donna's weight. Donna, unaware still of the danger behind them, giggled and patted Emma's face encouragingly. Fear accelerated Emma's pulse, gave unknown strength to her legs and lungs. She ran as she had never run before, clutching Donna protectively. Behind her came the bull, gathering speed as his massive weight thundered down upon them. Soon she could hear him.

His breath sounded agonisingly loud. Or was that her own breath, coming so painfully?

Clutched against her, Donna could not see the bull, but she suddenly seemed to become aware of the danger, perhaps in some peculiar telepathic leap between their two minds. The little body grew rigid. The little hands clutched fearfully.

'All right ...' Emma panted reassuringly, feeling far from certain that they would reach the gate. 'Don't be afraid, darling.'

The gate blurred in front of her. She flung herself upward, Donna held forward out of all danger.

Afterwards she never could remember exactly

how she climbed the gate. One moment she was on the wrong side, the bull bearing down upon her. The next she was falling forward, hands out in an effort to stop herself, but at least safely on the right side of the gate with the bull swerving away, angrily cheated, on the other side.

Head swimming, lungs rasping, she reached for Donna. 'Are you all right, darling?'

But Donna was laughing. 'Emma all dirty!'

A car screeched to a halt beside them. Dazedly, Emma saw Ross leap out, come at a run, his face pale. He knelt beside her, looked from one to the other, looked at the bull snorting and pawing the muddy ground in the field beyond.

'My God, what happened?'

'Don't ask ...' Emma tried to laugh, wondering if that was really her own blood pouring down her sleeve, and where it could be coming from.

'You've cut your arm,' he said, raising it to inspect the wound.

'Only a graze,' she said, aware with astonishment that for some impossible reason it gave her a pang of pleasure to see his head bent to look at her, his eyes resting on her without hostility.

'The cow ran at us,' Donna said waveringly.

'Did it, indeed?' said Ross in grim tones.

Emma looked up at him, grimaced. 'My fault. I'm sorry—I should have stayed with her all the time.'

'I know how it happened,' he said. 'Mrs Pat rang me. I came back at once. It was nobody's fault—

children will wander off, and no one can watch three children at once.'

'Emma's dirty,' said Donna, assuming disapproval now that Ross, the stern male, was present.

Emma involuntarily laughed. 'I'm naughty,' she agreed in a light voice.

Ross lifted her to her feet, his hands firm on her arms. 'I'll run you both home. I should think your legs are aching after a gallop across a field with Bonaparte after you!'

'Is that really his name?' Emma laughed, thinking how well it suited the bull.

'It is—they call him Nappy for short.' He cocked an eye at Donna, who giggled. 'Ah, here comes Tracy. She can be our little messenger and convey the good news to Mrs Pat and Edie. They're out of their minds with anxiety.'

Tracy gave Donna a cross, reproving stare. 'Where have you been? You'll get a smack. We've been looking for you for ages, and Edie's crying like a waterworks ...' Becoming conscious of Ross's glance, she added primly, 'Mrs Pat said like a waterworks.'

'Skip back and tell them we've found Donna and she's quite safe,' Ross said. 'Ask Edie to bring you and Robin back to the cottage right away, will you? Time you three had a bath and were off to bed, I think. You've had a busy day again today.'

'Why is Emma all black?' Tracy asked, staring. 'Did she fall in a puddle?'

'Yes,' said Ross. 'Now, be off with you.'

Tracy ran off reluctantly. Ross handed Donna

into the car, and Emma got in beside her, aware of a faintly distasteful odour.

'The cowshed fragrance stems from yourself, I'm afraid,' Ross told her, tongue in cheek, seeing her wrinkling her nose.

She looked down at her best black-and-red check dress, with its flared skirt and patent leather belt. A groan of horror and grief came from her as she saw what had happened to it when she fell, and then a groan of disgust as she realised what she had fallen into.

'I shall have to scrub myself until my skin is raw to get rid of this smell,' she said with anguish. 'My tights are ruined, and look at my shoes!' surveying them with dismay.

Ross chuckled. 'Never mind. Put it down to experience, and remember, you've had what you might call a baptism of fire.' His eyes twinkled at the wrath reflected in her face. 'Country living isn't as hygienic as life in town, you know. We aren't all plastic-wrapped and tidy. The only smell in a town is the reek of petrol fumes, I think. Personally, I prefer the smell of a horse or a cow, but tastes differ.'

'Emma ran and ran,' Donna said admiringly. 'Then we fell over the gate.'

Ross shot Emma a look in the driving mirror. 'Quite the little heroine,' he drawled.

She flushed. 'Oh, shut up!'

Ross took charge of Donna when they arrived. The child was unscratched, comparatively clean, since Emma had instinctively protected her from the fall without even knowing what she was doing. Ross stood her at the kitchen sink on a chair and let her play contentedly with the water in a plastic bowl. Emma went upstairs to take a bath.

Later, scrubbed clean and wearing jeans and a sweater, she came downstairs with her dirty clothes in a little parcel, rolled up together. 'I must do some washing. The sooner these are clean the better!'

Ross surveyed her with mocking amusement. 'Town dweller!'

'I notice you always wash thoroughly after you've been at work in a barn,' she snapped.

'A matter of common sense,' he shrugged. 'More hygienic.'

'Don't tell me you actually like the smell of manure,' she protested incredulously.

He grinned. 'Not on myself,' he admitted unashamedly.

'I thought so,' she tossed her head in triumph.

He moved closer, looked down at her face, at the clear, healthy skin, aglow with colour, at the wide, warm eyes the colour of chestnuts, at the generous pink mouth and rounded chin.

'You smell a lot nicer now,' he said, sniffing the fragrance of bath salts and talc. 'Like a garden.'

Emma was hypnotised, fixed by his unwavering grey eyes, held like a rabbit under their spell.

'Thank you,' she said huskily, with an effort.

His face moved closer, as if involuntarily. Their eyes held. Then they heard Edie's voice outside, heard Robin's busy little feet hurrying along the path.

The moment shattered. They drew apart, both rather flushed. Emma lifted Donna from her chair at the sink, and Ross turned to greet the others. Time flowed on again.

CHAPTER FIVE

'WE haven't discussed the subject of compensation yet,' Ross said a day later, as he and Emma amicably pruned the roses together while Edie took the children for a walk down the road to see Mrs Pat.

Emma's smooth brow wrinkled. 'Compensation?' She connected the word, not surprisingly, with the accident. 'I think Judith will have to get in touch with my insurance company, won't she? I was fully insured, thank goodness.'

'Not for Judith,' he said, grinning. 'For you, fathead.'

'Me?' She stared. 'I wasn't hurt!'

'Compensation for looking after the children,' he said patiently. 'A weekly wage, a salary—call it what you like. You're doing a great job. Judith will be very grateful. When I visited her yesterday she asked me to mention it to you—she left it to you to decide what sum to fix.'

'I don't want money,' she protested, horrified.

'Nonsense, of course you must be paid. Why should you do all this for nothing?'

'Two reasons,' she said coolly. 'Number one, I

feel responsible for the accident. Number two, I'm having the time of my life. I ought to pay you. I'm having free board and lodging, an enchanting holiday, and I have the pleasure of looking after three adorable children. I haven't enjoyed myself like this for years.'

'You're a very surprising girl, do you know that?' He studied her like a scientist with some rare species of insect under his microscope. 'Look, are you sure about this?'

'Certain,' she said firmly.

He shrugged. 'Well, I'll leave the subject for the moment. No doubt Judith will have something to say when you see her.'

'Is it arranged that I take the children in to see her on Sunday, then?' she asked.

They had had a little difficulty over arranging for the children to visit their mother. She had been moved into an open ward, and small children were discouraged from visiting, since they might see sights which would disturb them.

Ross nodded. 'Just for five minutes, the ward Sister insisted. I think both Judith and the children need to have this visit, so I pressed hard for her to agree to it, or I think she would have been more difficult.'

'The children are secretly a bit worried about their mother,' Emma agreed. 'I hope that a visit, however short, will reassure them a little. Particularly Donna ... She may be very young, but that makes it harder for her to understand what's happening.'

The gate creaked open behind them, and they turned. Amanda stood there, immaculate as ever in a cashmere twin set, creamy pearls and a misty blue tweed skirt.

'What a glorious afternoon,' she said, giving Ross one of her bright, admiring smiles.

Emma returned to her pruning, snipping away energetically as if her life depended upon it.

'Your nanny seems a little over-enthusiastic with those clippers,' Amanda drawled, delighted to put Emma into the wrong.

'Hey!' Ross grinned. 'Leave something on the bush, won't you?'

'I'll show you,' Amanda said sweetly, deftly removing the clippers from Emma's fingers before she realised what was happening. 'We know something about pruning, don't we, Ross?' She turned her attention to one of the standards, a soft apricot rose with damask petals and a mass of blooms. Emma reluctantly had to admit that Amanda certainly did know what she was doing. She pruned fast, but precisely.

Ross watched wryly, hands on hips. Amanda glanced up at him, her sapphire blue eyes gleaming gently. 'The gardens at Queen's Daumaury are looking their best just now, I think.' She spoke very softly, her tone curiously insidious, as though she trod on delicate ground. 'The roses are still in full bloom, but the shrubberies are so colourful. The buddleias!'

'I'm no gardener,' Ross cut in tersely. 'I keep this place tidy when I have time, but that's my limit. I'll go and see if Edie has put the kettle on.'

'I just saw her down at that public house,' said Amanda sharply.

Ross looked blank, as though he had forgotten. 'Well then, I'll put the kettle on myself.'

'No, let me,' said Emma sweetly. 'You stay and talk to Amanda, Ross.'

He gave her a wrathful glance, but unmoved, she left them together and went into the house.

Ross, joined her later, alone. She gave him a secret, amused little glance, then asked innocently, 'Oh, where's Amanda? Didn't she want any tea?' She had laid out shortcake on a rose-strewn plate, placed three cups on a tray.

'No, she did not,' Ross said shortly.

'Well, you do surprise me,' Emma murmured, eyes lowered to hide the gleam of amusement.

He shot her an unsmiling look. 'Don't be funny with me, Emma. I'm not in a humorous vein.'

She lifted her eyes to his dark face, a dimple at the side of her pink mouth. 'Why, you do sound fierce!' Laughter brimmed in the warm brown eyes.

He took her suddenly by the elbows, shook her vehemently. 'You little cat! How dare you make fun of me?' But he was not as grim as he sounded, the grey eyes held a smile as he looked down into her upturned face.

'Amanda's very lovely,' Emma said with apparent irrelevance.

'Oh, exquisite,' he nodded. 'Like a Dresden shepherdess, fragile and lovely and very, very expensive.'

'Is she a member of the Daumaury family?'

Emma asked, wondering if Ross avoided Amanda because he felt her to be above his touch, a bright star forever out of his reach.

He turned away from her and stared out of the latticed windows at the bright, sunlit garden. 'Yes,' he said curtly.

'Is she Leon Daumaury's granddaughter?'

'I'm not certain what the exact relationship is,' Ross said brusquely. 'I think she's his great-niece, but it may not be as close as that.'

'Do her parents live at the house, too?'

'They're dead,' said Ross.

'Oh...' Emma looked upset. 'Poor Amanda! How very sad.'

Ross shrugged. 'It was years ago. She got over it long ago.'

'Does one ever get over things like that? There must always be a gap.'

'What about you?' He looked at her. 'Your parents? Still alive?'

She smiled. 'Of course, and very busy. My father's a doctor in Norfolk, a rather remote village practice. My mother breeds Siamese cats. I've got three brothers and a sister, all married, and five nephews and a niece.' Her brown eyes were filled with loving warmth. 'We're a close sort of family. I'm the only one who left Norfolk, in fact.'

'You left to take up your art training, I suppose?'

'Yes. I had no option. London is the best place to train, although, of course, I could have gone to an art college locally.'

'But you were eager to taste big city life?' His voice was gently mocking.

She laughed. 'Something like that.'

'So you're country bred, after all,' he murmured. 'Why didn't you say so before? Why let me go on making false assumptions about you?'

She gave him a sparkling glance. 'Perhaps it will teach you not to jump to conclusions about people in future!'

He pinched her cheek. 'Miss Impudence! Do you have a flat in London?'

'Yes,' she said.

'Share it, or live alone?'

Her eyes lifted, wide and innocent. 'Share it, actually.'

'Oh? Is your flatmate nice?'

'What a lot of questions you ask,' said Emma sweetly. 'Very nice, as a matter of fact.'

He grimaced. 'I see. The flow of information now ceases, does it? Am I treading on very private ground?' His eyes were sharp as they rested on her face.

She laughed. 'I can see that imagination of yours working away again! No, it isn't private ground. I share my flat with a friend of mine called Fanny— she's a secretary, works for a publisher. She's very pretty, a blonde, and very sweet. We've shared the flat for two years. Any more questions?'

'The obvious one,' he said coolly.

Her eyes opened very wide. 'Oh? What's that?'

'Where's the man in your life?' he asked.

She was silent for a second, then said calmly, 'There isn't one at present.'

He watched her. 'At present,' he repeated.

Emma had a sudden image of Guy, his face dappled by sunshine under silver birch trees, agile and healthy in tennis clothes, smiling at her. She half-closed her eyes, waiting for pain to tear at her heart, but felt only calm acceptance. Her eyes opened again, a frown of relieved disbelief gathering on her brow.

Ross was still watching her closely. 'Has it been over long?' he asked gently.

She looked at him, astonished, and found herself answering without hesitation. 'Not long.'

'It was serious? For you, at least?'

'I thought so,' she said, still incredulously testing her own feelings.

'And for him?'

'No, never for him, although I thought so, but that wasn't his fault, it was mine,' she answered incoherently.

'He must have given you cause to think so,' said Ross coldly.

She shook her head. 'No. Oh, no. We were friends.' She looked at him appealingly. 'That is possible, you know—friendship between a man and a woman, without strings.'

'In your case it wasn't without strings, apparently,' he replied sardonically.

'Guy didn't realise...'

'He was a fool,' said Ross.

Emma was about to protest, but in her heart of

hearts she knew that she agreed with him. Guy must have been blind not to see what was happening to her.

'How did it end?' Ross asked curiously.

Flatly, she said, 'Fanny came home from America and...'

'I get the picture,' Ross interrupted, hearing the echo of old pain in her voice.

Emma looked at him. 'Do you know, I regret Fanny far more than I regret Guy ... perhaps soon I'll be able to face her again.'

'Is that why you came down here?' He spoke sharply.

She nodded.

'It was that recent?' Ross demanded.

'It seems like a million years ago,' she said wonderingly. 'Isn't that strange? Sometimes time drags on for years, and nothing seems to happen. Then suddenly time telescopes, and things happen one after the other, giving you no pause for rest, so that you feel quite dazed and disorientated. Fanny and I shared that flat for two years. We dated, we enjoyed ourselves, we worked hard. But nothing really happened ... do you know what I mean? It was all very peaceful. Then Fanny went away, and I met Guy and fell for him hard. Fanny came back and I saw their faces ... it was like watching two clouds collide—the flash of electricity almost blinded me. I had to get away, so I came down here, only to crash into your sister and find myself, incredibly enough, playing nanny to three children. Sometimes I wonder if this is all real!'

'It's real,' Ross said in a hard voice. 'So you came down here to mend a broken heart?'

'I came to escape from an intolerable situation,' she said, not liking the tone of his voice. 'Fanny and Guy went around smelling like orange blossom all day I couldn't stand it.'

'A sad story,' he said mockingly.

'If you'd ever been in love you wouldn't use that tone of voice,' she said angrily.

'What makes you think I haven't?' he asked sardonically.

She raised wide eyes to his face. 'Well, have you? You've just heard my life story. Is there to be no quid pro quo?'

'Quid pro quo,' he murmured, grinning. 'A fair return, in other words? Why not? You satisfied my curiosity, and you've been impressively discreet yourself, despite everything. Well, then, yes, I've been in love ... once or twice, as a matter of fact. When I was eighteen with a girl I met at college— a fellow student, who was kind but distant, and wanted to pursue her career, not marry me. I fell out of love as fast as I fell in, to tell the truth.'

She sighed. 'I know what you mean. Sometimes I wonder if love exists at all. I've been briefly in love now and then—it was fun, but very temporary.' Then she looked at him, smiling. 'Sorry, I interrupted. What was the other time you fell in love?'

He looked at her, hard. 'You don't know?'

'Why should I?' She was puzzled.

'Oh, village gossip, for one thing,' he said.

'I don't listen to it, and anyway, there hasn't been any.'

'Oh, there's gossip,' he said tartly. 'You just haven't heard it.' He moved towards the window, stood, his hands in his pockets, staring out. 'I met her at a dance. She was very beautiful and sweet, with big innocent blue eyes, like a child. I was knocked for six. It was obvious to everyone that I was serious, I suppose, and her family took it for granted that we would marry. We saw each other all the time, and gradually I ... well, it sounds brutally hard, but I found that she bored me. She was silly, shallow, rather selfish. She came to stay at my home. My family approved of the marriage. But I felt I had to make it plain to her that I'd changed my mind. I told her one night ... she cried and begged me to ... Oh, hell, it was murder! She was in debt. Her family had spent money on clothes for her, money they couldn't afford ... I was sorry for her. I offered to pay her bills, but I would not marry her.'

Emma was very still, shocked by the story, wondering if the girl in question was Amanda Craig, but then surely it could not be, for Amanda lived at Queen's Daumaury, and must have plenty of money.

Ross went on harshly, 'I was glad to get to bed that night, I can tell you. Around midnight I was woken up, though. It was her—she'd come to plead with me once more. She began to cry, to sob loudly. She ran out of my room, and I followed her, trying to comfort her. She ran into her own room and I turned back, but she began to scream like a train whistle. The next moment there were half a dozen people staring accusingly at me, and she appeared, her nightdress torn on the shoulder, her hair all over the place, accusing me of attempted seduction...'

Emma was indignant. 'Well, what a beastly trick!'

He swung, looked at her closely, his grey eyes searching her face. 'Thank you,' he said deeply.

'For what?' She was puzzled.

'For believing me.'

'Of course I believe you,' she said warmly. 'No one who knew you would believe that you were capable of forcible seduction of a girl under your own roof!'

'My ... my family believed it,' Ross said in a harsh voice.

'They didn't?'

'They not only believed her story, they threw me out on the strength of it, and regarded me as a monster.'

'What, Judith, too?' She was incredulous.

'Not Judith, no. She always said the story was laughable.'

'Mrs Pat wouldn't believe it, either,' said Emma thoughtfully, remembering certain cryptic remarks, and now able to interpret them in the light of Ross's explanation. She gave him a little grin. 'No wonder you didn't want me moving into the cottage unless you had a chaperone! Once bitten, twice shy!'

He nodded. 'It was nothing personal, you understand. Just a sense of self-preservation.'

'I can well understand it!' She shuddered. 'It leaves a nasty taste in the mouth, although in a way I feel sorry for her. She may have been in love with you and felt so desperate she lost her mind, temporarily, and prepared to do anything to keep you.'

He grimaced. 'If you loved someone would you do "anything"? I've never accepted this modern theory that "love" excuses any crime, however beastly. From what you just told me about yourself and this Guy of yours, I imagine you would draw the line at stooping so low, too.'

Emma sighed. 'Perhaps I wasn't as much in love with Guy as this girl with you? Who knows?'

'Don't make excuses for her,' he snapped. 'I fancy love was not the motive. Money came first. She was desperate, all right—desperate for money.'

'You're very cynical,' she said, half indulgently. 'I suppose it's only natural after such an experience.'

'And you?' he asked. 'Are you cynical about men after your experience of love?'

'Why should I be? Guy was always straight with me. I fooled myself, I wasn't fooled by Guy. And believe me, he fell in love with Fanny at first sight— even though I was on the losing side I could see that.' She looked dubious. 'But it's true that I shall be extra cautious in future. I'm not going to be in any hurry to fall in love again. This mouse stays clear of traps in future.'

Ross laughed. 'What a funny little creature you are!'

'Why, thanks,' she said, offended. 'Glad I amuse you.'

This only made him laugh louder.

Emma felt, after this conversation, that she and Ross had achieved a new relationship, friendly and understanding, based on mutual trust. It was something of a shock, therefore, when very shortly after this she found herself once more at odds with him.

She took the children over to visit their mother in the hospital. Judith was looking much better, and her face lit up when she saw the three children coming towards her. When she had hugged each one, she looked at Emma with a smile. 'How can I think you?'

'Nothing to thank me for,' said Emma casually.

'Ross has done nothing but sing your praises,' Judith added firmly. 'I don't know what we would have done without you.'

'Have you forgotten who got you into this mess?'

'That dog!' Judith capped with a twinkle.

Emma laughed. 'Well, yes, but I wasn't thinking fast enough.'

'All the same, I'm grateful,' Judith insisted. 'The children look marvellous.'

'Emma's a good cook,' said Robin in his cool little voice. 'Even Uncle Ross says so.'

Judith's eyes met Emma's. 'Even Uncle Ross!' Judith murmured in complete understanding. 'My word, that's praise indeed!'

Emma giggled.

'How is he bearing up under the strain of playing host to a horde of kids?' asked Judith.

'Bravely,' said Emma.

'Hmm...'

'Is it true we've got a grandfather?' Robin asked suddenly.

There was a taut silence. Judith looked at him, then at Emma, her face pale, her eyes enquiring.

Emma was not sure how to respond, but was saved the problem by Robin, who added, 'Tracy says we have. We saw him in a big car, he stared at us, but he didn't say anything. He's old and small...'

Suddenly there were bright tears in Judith's eyes, and she turned her head hurriedly aside. Emma was appalled. She looked out of the window for inspiration, saw an icecream van standing beside the back gate of the hospital. 'Goodness, look! An icecream van! When we leave, we'll stop and buy one, shall we? Oh, dear, here's Sister, coming to turn us out, I'm afraid. You must all kiss Mummy goodbye. She'll be coming home soon now, so it won't be for long.'

Judith hugged them all, under Sister's approving eye, and Emma gave her a quick, apologetic smile. Judith's eyes were still damp and she looked pale.

'Thanks,' she whispered again as Emma left.

That evening, when the children were safety tucked up, Emma looked across the sitting-room at Ross, nodding sleepily over the detective story he was reading.

After their chat recently, she felt less apprehensive about bringing up the subject, but it was still not an easy one for her to broach. She did not know all the circumstances, but she felt that someone ought to say something.

'When we were at the hospital today——' she began uneasily.

Ross looked up. 'Hum...? Yes?

'Robin mentioned Leon Daumaury to Judith and she began to cry. Isn't there anything to be done about that situation? It seems a pity for a family to be split like this.'

'So you do listen to gossip, after all,' he said unpleasantly, standing up abruptly.

'No,' she protested. 'It's just that...'

'Just that like most women you can't help interfering in things that don't concern you! Well, I'll thank you to keep out of my affairs, and that includes my sister's life, too. You're here to look after the children, not play the social worker and solve old problems. You know nothing of the background, you know nothing of the people involved. So mind your own business, Miss Leigh!'

He strode out of the room, snatching his jacket from the hall and banging out of the house.

Emma stared at the fire, her face flushed and full of wrath. Really, he was impossible! How dared he speak to her like that! She had only meant to... She sighed. The road to Hell was supposed to be paved with good intentions, wasn't it? Perhaps she had been rather presumptuous in imagining that she could solve an old family quarrel overnight.

All the same, there was no need for Ross to speak to her in that brutal fashion. He was a beast. I detest him, she told herself. I really detest him.

CHAPTER SIX

EACH morning the children walked down to chat to two donkeys, Barnaby and Jessie, and feed them sugar lumps. Jessie was all big-eyed eagerness, gentle and nuzzling. Barnaby was pushy, greedy and determined to get more than his fair share. Emma loved to watch the children with them, seeing how the animals revealed their true nature, seeing how the children reacted instinctively to it.

Mrs Pat often said, 'I don't know why I keep them, eating their heads off ... but I haven't the heart to sell them. I won them in a raffle at the village fête a few years back. The donkey farm up along had given the Vicar two donkeys to raffle. I bought a ticket because I never win raffles, but blow me down if I didn't win this one ... now in the old days it would have been a pig. We always had a pig at the village fête—bowled for it, we did. Winner got the pig. Useful animals, pigs. You can eat every bit of them.'

'Oh, Mrs Pat,' said Tracy reproachfully. 'How horrid!'

'Horrid, indeed! Who loves a bacon sandwich for her tea?' Mrs Pat teased.

'But that isn't a pig,' Tracy said in a muddled way. 'Not a pig I know, I mean. Not one I've won at bowling. That comes from a shop and I didn't know it.'

They all laughed gently at her. 'I know just what you mean,' Emma agreed. 'When I was five years old I won a chick at a fair. They were giving them away instead of goldfish. I put it in a drawer from my mother's kitchen cabinet. I lined it with straw and put it by the kitchen stove when the chick would be nice and warm. My father said it would die, but it didn't. It grew and grew until it had to move out into the garden with the other hens. But it always was tamer than the others, more friendly. I called it Clara Cluck. But next Christmas my father sold the hens to a butcher in the village, and I cried all night. I knew, of course, that a hen isn't a real pet, not like a dog or a cat, but Clara Cluck was a person to me ... I wouldn't eat chicken for months.'

Ross watched her, his expression baffling. 'Just as well your father wasn't a farmer,' he said.

'Talking of fairs,' said Mrs Pat, watching them both with interest, 'there's one at Moscombe Down this week.'

'Oh, can we go?' Tracy flared into white-faced excitement. 'Oh, please, Uncle Ross, Emma ... I love fairs. If we go I can have a ride on the round-about with the horses ... I love to ride them and go up and down and round and round.'

'I like fairs!' Donna cried, clapping her small hands and jumping up and down on tiptoes.

Robin looked intensely at his uncle, as if silently begging him to agree.

Ross laughed. 'Why not? I enjoy a good fair myself.'

'When? Tonight?' demanded Robin, always desiring certainties.

Ross shrugged. 'Is it open?'

Mrs Pat nodded.

'Then tonight it shall be,' Ross nodded, smiling at Robin.

The fair was small but noisy. As they approached it in the car they could both see and hear it—the vivid flare of the electric lights over the stalls, the coloured bulbs winking around the rides, the gay painted colours of the horses and the ostriches on the merry-go-round—and the loud swirl of the music blaring out from the various mechanical organs.

It was set up in a field at Moscombe Down, just outside the village itself, and many cars were parked in the next field. A farmer's son sat wrapped in an old black duffle coat taking a few pence from each car as it slowly drove into the temporary car park.

They parked and walked back to the fair. Already it was pretty crowded. Vans selling icecream, candy floss, hot-dogs and tea stood on the perimeter of the field. Then came an inner circle of stalls—coconut shy, darts, rifle booth, plate smashing, a rather shabby Ghost Train and a Haunted House, and a large amusement arcade tent already thronged with teenage boys busily throwing away their pennies on clanging pinball machines. In the very centre stood the main attractions, the dodgem cars, the big wheel, the Chair-o-Plane, the merry-go-rounds. There was one for small children with cars, buses and stage coaches going round. There was a bigger one with blue-and-silver horses and bright yellow ostriches going round. There was another one with very up-to-date space rockets going round.

The aisles were crowded, the grass already torn and trampled back to mud. Children scampered along with bright, rosy faces in which the lights of the stall were reflected like fireworks. Emma and Ross firmly restrained the three small children. 'It's easy to get lost in this crowd, so stay close to us, and if you do get separated, go to the dodgem car stand and wait there until one of us comes. Do you understand?'

All three nodded, half listening, eyes wide and filled with brightness.

Ross grinned. 'Well, O.K., let it rip ... which do you want to go on first ...?'

Three different answers came, all panted eagerly. Emma laughed. 'I'll take Donna on the little merry-go-round. You take Tracy and Robin on the horses.'

Donna proudly took her seat in a big red London bus, seized the driving wheel and noisily clanged the bell rope which hung down beside her. The music started. The merry-go-round began to turn slowly.

Emma stood and waved. Behind her she heard the music of the other one. She glanced over her shoulder. Ross was riding a bright yellow ostrich, holding the slippery barley-sugar pole with one hand while the other held Robin in front of him. Tracy sat raptly on a shimmering silver-blue horse whose white mane flowed like moonlight in the lights.

Ross looked across at her and winked. She smiled back. She envied the children. They were lost in wonderland, bright-eyed in the land of dreams. She could remember how it felt, but she could no longer quite share that old enchantment. She still loved the fair, but faith no longer sealed her eyes against the realisation of how shabby the stalls were, how tawdry the paints and gildings on the merry-go-round. Adulthood made one too critical, perhaps.

When she had helped Donna off the bus, Ross joined her, holding Robin's hand. 'How about some candy floss?' he suggested.

The children eagerly acclaimed the idea. Later, gingerly nibbling at the fluffy aureole of the pink cloud she held, Emma felt a bubble of laughter welling up in her throat. I'm happy, she thought. I'm deliriously happy! I was never this happy with Guy! Then her mind pulled up with a jerk. What am I saying? What am I thinking?

She looked at Ross. He was already half-way through his candy floss. Some had stuck to his nose, leaving a sugary pink streak across it. He looked at her, grinning.

'There's pink sugar on your nose,' she said.

'Does it suit me?' he asked cheerfully.

She considered. 'I think it does, rather. Makes you less grim, less the ogre.'

'Ogre?' He flipped a derisive eyebrow. 'Was I ever that?'

'From the first second,' she said firmly.

'What does that make you?' He pretended to study her, his grey gaze thoughtful on her glowing pink cheeks, warm brown eyes and windblown hair. 'The good fairy?' He shook his head. 'You look more like Brown Owl.'

'Hoot hoot...' offered Donna helpfully.

They all laughed.

The dodgem cars were popular, but Emma found them a little too violent, and Donna soon grew tense, so she and Donna were glad to retire to the sidelines to watch the others from a safe distance, hearing Robin shriek with glee at each tremendous bump, hearing Tracy shout fiercely, 'Bump him, Uncle!'

They had a go on each stall, each ride, before they finally agreed to call it a day and leave for home. As the evening wore on the crowds grew thicker. People had come from miles away. There was so little entertainment in the country, one had to seize one's chances of a little fun while one could.

When they left it was pitch dark. They edged their way out of the car park and headed for home. Donna was fast asleep on Emma's comfortable lap. Robin was sleepily curled up in the circle of her arm. Tracy sat beside Ross, chattering to him, still keyed up with excitement over her evening.

When the children were in bed Emma made supper. Edie had gone down to the pub to help her sister for an hour or two, by special arrangement, and wouldn't be back until ten o'clock. Emma fried eggs, bacon, mushrooms, tomatoes and bread. Ross made the tea and laid the table in the kitchen. 'Cosier, as there are just the two of us,' he said.

They sat companionably opposite each other, both quite hungry after the hours in the cold night air. The smell of the food was ambrosial. Ross sighed.

'I've never been so ravenous! You're a born home-maker, Emma.'

She felt her cheeks glow with pleasure.

They had just finished their meal, leaning back with sighs of contentment, when Amanda appeared in the doorway. Her sapphire blue glance skimmed the room, the loaded table, their faces, the intimacy of the setting.

'Am I interrupting anything?' she asked icily.

Ross looked at her lazily. 'You just missed the meal of the century,' he said. 'Simple but utterly satisfying.'

'How nice.' Her voice was glacial. She looked at the plates and a grimace of distaste twisted her lovely features. 'Fried food? How fattening! I detest it.'

'Perhaps if you have a tough job of work to do you would grow to like it,' Ross said calmly. 'I put in a solid day's work, so I need a good solid meal when I get home.'

'I work!' Amanda looked furious. 'I'm by no means idle.'

'You arrange flowers in a bowl, you choose dinner menus, you make phone calls,' said Ross in lightly disparaging tones. 'You don't call that work, do you?'

She was tight-lipped now, her cheeks sporting a hard red coin of colour. 'That isn't all I do! And anyway, I think it's wrong to take on a job if you don't need to do so—you're taking bread out of other people's mouths. What would be the point of me working at some boring nine-to-five job for a few pounds a week? I don't need the money and other people do.' She gave Ross a long, reproachful glare. 'I don't know how you can do what you do, Ross. I really don't.'

'I do a useful job of work and I get paid accordingly. That satisfies my independence and my pride,' he said.

She looked at him from under her long lashes. 'Oh, your pride,' she said softly.

He flushed and stood up abruptly. Emma watched them with a sense of uneasiness. She sensed something behind this brief exchange, something she did not understand. Ross might make unpleasant remarks about Amanda, he might pretend to avoid her and distrust her, but whenever she saw them together she was struck by an intimacy, a silent understanding which ran below the surface of their talk.

'I'll help you wash up, Emma,' he said, turning towards her.

'No,' Amanda said quickly. 'Ross, why don't I help you wash up while Emma takes a well-earned rest? She deserves it, I'm sure. She looks tired.'

Ross surveyed Emma's face. 'Yes,' he said, in surprise, 'you are looking a trifle worn. Amanda's right.'

Emma smiled with difficulty. 'Thanks,' she said. 'I'll go up to my room, if you're sure . . .'

'Of course,' he said, watching her leave the room with some bewilderment. 'Funny! She looked fine earlier.'

'Really?' Amanda smiled sweetly. 'It caught up with her, though. Those children can be exhausting.'

'Yes.' But Ross looked concerned still.

Emma sank down on her bed and looked at herself grimly in the dressing-table mirror. You look like death warmed up, she told herself. You look like a girl who just found out she was in love again, and in love with the wrong man again, to boot. Honestly, Emma Leigh, you are a fool! How could you be so stupid as to fall for Ross?

In the mirror her brown eyes looked wearily at her, astonished yet strangely resigned. In love with Ross? Was she? Really? She groped for memories of Guy and found them elusive, misty, like dissolving shadows. She had never been in love with Guy at all. There had been a brief enchantment, compounded of summer sunshine, laughter and shared fun—the way she felt about Ross bore no comparison with how she had felt about Guy.

She grimaced at herself. Who was kidding whom? Perhaps in a few weeks she would wonder what all the fuss was about . . . she would grope for memories of Ross and find them gone.

Am I a sort of emotional dodgem car? she asked

herself. Bouncing on a rebound from man to man?

She heard Ross's voice outside in the garden; deep, serious, endearingly concerned. Emma winced. The brown eyes looked at her from the mirror gravely. Oh, I'm in love this time, she thought miserably. There's no heady summer sunshine magic about this ... it's far too painful, far too real.

There was one common factor, though—once more she had fallen in love with a man who only had eyes for another girl. Whatever it was that came between Ross and Amanda, one thing was pretty clear—Ross was unable to break away from her. He might despise her for her attitudes, mock her wealth, her flower-arranging, her snobbishness; but he was trapped in a net and he knew it. Amanda could always make him come when she whistled.

If that isn't love, what is? Emma asked herself. Then, with a sigh, she turned away from her reflection and began to get ready for bed.

Over breakfast, Ross said, 'A fine brisk autumn morning ... I feel like riding.' He looked at Emma with challenge in his eyes, a faint, mocking smile on his mouth. 'What about you? Care to try a canter?'

'Is there a riding stable near here?' She glanced at the three children, intent upon their meal. 'What about the children? Do any of them ride?'

'Edie can take them down to Mrs Pat for the day,' he said.

She looked doubtful. 'It might not be convenient for Mrs Pat. I wouldn't like to ask too much of her.

She's been so kind, I would hate her to begin to resent me.'

'I've already talked it over with her,' Ross said indulgently. 'You ought to get away from the children now and again. Everyone needs a break. Mrs Pat offered voluntarily, I promise you. In fact, it was her idea that you should have some relaxation. The horse riding was mine.'

Emma smiled. 'You're both very kind. Then I would love to go, in that case.'

'We can ride on Barnaby and Jessie one day if we're good,' said Robin, adding thoughtfully, 'If we want to. If we don't fall off.'

'Cautious little man, aren't you?' Ross teased him.

Robin dimpled. Donna said dreamily, 'Ride Jessie...' Clearly the idea appealed to her, despite Robin's wary reservations. Tracy, munching buttered toast, looked up and said crisply, 'Donna's too little. It will just be Robin and me. I'll ride Barnaby, Robin can ride Jessie.'

Donna began to cry with the full-throated abandon of babyhood. Emma flashed Tracy a cross look and cuddled the smaller child to her lovingly. 'Donna shall ride Jessie if she wants to ... a few moments round the field won't hurt her. Ross can hold her on! Jessie will walk for Ross.'

'Thanks,' Ross said cheerfully. He looked at Donna's wet-eyed appeal. 'All right, dumpling! Uncle Ross will take you to ride on Jessie tomorrow morning!'

Donna gave Tracy a triumphant, damp smile,

and Tracy finished her toast in silence.

Trying to placate her, Emma asked her to help with the washing up. Ross vanished with the other two children. Tracy's stiff-necked silence only held out for a short while against Emma's coaxing. A little judicious praise, a smile or two, and Tracy was cheerful once more, eager to demonstrate her skill with the tea-towel. They put the breakfast things away together in all amity.

Mrs Pat was pleased to see the children. As usual, her garden was alive with flapping washing, the hens were contentedly scratching and squawking and her small black kitten was perched on a low branch above the fence, arching and spitting as it eyed a stray dog which was barking at it from the lane.

'There's so much to do at Mrs Pat's,' Tracy said with a sigh of content, racing up the garden with Robin and Donna in her wake.

Mrs Pat beamed at Ross and Emma. 'Off to ride, then?' She looked with approval at Emma's sturdy blue jeans. 'That's right, you enjoy yourself. Worked well with the children, hasn't she, Ross?' And her gaze challenged him to hesitate with his response.

He grinned. 'What am I expected to say? Of course she's worked well with them. A proper tower of strength, as you've said before, Mrs Pat. I'm sure Judith is very grateful.'

Emma laughed. Mrs Pat shook her head reprovingly at him. Edie, who was still shy with him, had scuttled into the kitchen and they heard her getting down cups and banging the kettle about. Mrs Pat said a hasty goodbye and vanished to find her sister.

'Mrs Pat would like to hear me give you a glowing testimonial,' Ross said mockingly. 'Shall I?'

Emma walked off. Over her shoulder, as he came after her, she said coolly, 'Don't bother.'

'Now you're offended,' he said, catching up with her.

'Everything I've done has been done for the sake of the children,' she said calmly, 'and for your sister. I don't want anything from you, Ross.'

'I see,' he said in an odd tone.

'Do you? I hope you do,' she said, wondering why she felt the need, the positive need, to say all this, to make it clear to him ... to make what clear, though?

He looked down at her. She raised her eyes, brown and warm as shiny new chestnuts with the sun on them. They stared at each other for a very long time in silence. Ross's eyes were unreadable to her, but his eyes searched hers as though seeking and finding the answer to some question he did not wish her to know he was asking.

She looked away at last. 'You think too much about ulterior motives, Ross,' she said sadly.

'Do I? Perhaps I do,' he said.

'Oh, I know your experiences have sometimes been unhappy in that direction, but everyone isn't made the same way. You can't always be suspicious of other people. I couldn't live like that. I couldn't bear to be so constricted, so suspicious and remote. You have to open up to life, to give people the benefit of the doubt.'

'Is that what you're going to do?' His voice was serious and questioning. 'Are you going to risk another heartbreak, Emma? Another emotional tangle? Haven't you learnt your lesson?'

She thrust her hands into the pockets of her yellow wool jacket, thick fisherman's knit, warm and comforting. Her chin was up. 'That's what life is about,' she said. 'Risk-taking.'

'I remember you once said to me that you would be cautious in future. This mouse stays clear of traps, you said!'

'I was wrong,' Emma stated flatly.

Ross stood still, staring at her bent head and waiting until she lifted it and looked up at him. 'You are an amazing girl,' he said. 'You say that with such simplicity.'

She was puzzled. 'What?'

'You said that you were wrong ... no qualification, no excuse ... just the blunt statement of fact.' His smile was brilliant, heart-touching. 'I like that. It's a rare quality. Most people want to make excuses for themselves, even when they know they're in the wrong. They want to say yes, but ... You just fling the words out without any strings attached to them, just as you walked away at once when you realised how things were between your friend and your young man. That took guts, Emma. A lot of girls would have put up a fight for him, and there would have been a lot of pain for everyone concerned then.'

She was embarrassed. Praise to her face made her

want to run away. 'Where is this stable?' she asked huskily. 'Is it much further?'

He laughed. 'No, just up Bundle Lane.'

'Bundle Lane?' Eagerly she questioned the name. 'What a strange name!'

'About fifty years ago there was a house at the top of it which was owned by an old miser who bought bundles of old clothes and the usual portable objects people try to sell when they're hard up —he was a sort of pawnbroker,' Ross explained. 'When he died they found his house crammed with peculiar objects. He sold the rags to a dealer, but he often kept the china or glass, and some of the stuff was very valuable. Some of it was rubbishy, naturally. He had no relatives, so the house and all its contents were sold and the money went to the church. His will had been made years earlier, but he had been religious as a youth.'

'What did the church do with the money, I wonder?' Emma was desperately trying to keep the conversation on impersonal subjects.

Ross spoke calmly. 'They built a new stone wall around the churchyard ... presumably to keep the old man safely inside.'

Emma giggled, then frowned. 'That wasn't very kind. Where is the church? I haven't seen one.'

'It really belongs to the next village. It's twelfth century, in pretty poor shape structurally, and has a congregation of about six. It shares a vicar with the Boxrey church. That's how these tiny parishes survive these days.'

'I would like to see it,' said Emma. 'Twelfth-century? That's very early.'

'Oh, the Normans knew how to build. It's basically solid, but of course it needs repairs, and there's no money available. The church tower fund is always appealing for money. The village holds endless jumble sales, fêtes and sponsored events, but the church just eats up money. All these old buildings do. Look at Queen's ...' His voice cut off suddenly.

'Queen's Daumaury?' she finished, her voice rising to a question. 'But then its owner can afford to keep it up, can't he?'

'I suppose so,' said Ross distantly.

They walked up Bundle Lane fast. Sheep grazed quietly on either side of them. The larks sang high overhead. The sky was a bright, clear cloudless blue. Through a belt of trees Emma caught sight of a tower, square and grey, with an embattled air. That, she guessed, was the famous church which 'ate' money.

The stables were set back from the road, in a ramshackle house and yard, where a sturdy, fair-haired woman with a square-shaped face and spatulate hands was energetically pitchforking soiled straw from one of the looseboxes into a wooden wagon. She looked round and grinned at them.

'Oh, there you are, Ross! You've chosen a good morning for it.' She looked along the stables and raised her voice. 'Ted! Saddle Juniper and Marcy for me.'

A small, gnarled man darted from the end box

and looked at them crossly, then set to work.

'Ted still enjoying the job?' asked Ross.

'He likes the horses,' said the fair woman with amusement. 'But he hates the customers. Hates putting a saddle on ... If he had his way, those horses would just eat me out of house and home and never set a hoof out of the yard! He hates to see them work. I have to nag him from dawn to dusk about it. He just can't see that a working horse has to work.'

'He's a good man with horses, though,' said Ross.

'Oh, he knows his job,' she agreed. 'Or I wouldn't keep him.'

'That was why I recommended him,' Ross said. 'He was a first-rate groom, worked in the best stables in the country until he began to drink.'

'He only drinks in the evenings now,' the woman put in. 'If I caught him drinking before six o'clock, I told him, he would have to go. He knows I mean it.'

'Good,' Ross nodded.

Ted led out two horses, one a calm-eyed grey with odd dappling on her flanks and the other a bay with an impatient, nervous manner. Ross took the bay's bridle. 'Juniper for me, obviously. Marcy will be perfect for you, Emma.'

'Ridden before?' asked the fair woman. 'I'm Lucy Todd, by the way, as Ross is obviously never going to introduce us.'

'I'm Emma Leigh and I have ridden before,' she smiled.

Ross gave a crack of laughter. 'She's the sort of

creature who may well turn out to be a champion show jumper,' he said. 'She's apparently a talented artist, a first-rate cook, a wonderful children's nurse and a heroine to boot . . .'

Emma gave him a furious glare. 'Oh, shut up!' She swung herself up into the saddle, gathered up the reins and moved off.

Lucy Todd looked amused and interested. 'A heroine?' she asked Ross.

'She saved my smallest niece from an enraged bull the other day,' he informed her with a broad smile.

'She sounds quite a girl,' commented Lucy Todd, watching Emma's easy, relaxed yet stylish riding. 'Straight back, good hands, good seat . . . I think I would even trust her on Juniper.'

'Well, I wouldn't,' said Ross firmly. 'I don't even trust myself on Juniper. He's a devil, not a horse.'

'Why do you always choose him, then?' asked Lucy, grinning knowingly at him.

'Because no one, not even a horse, gets the better of me,' Ross explained.

He caught up with Emma, and side by side they moved off along the lane. There was a sandy bridle path through Boxrey Wood, winding a little at first, then straightening out into a downhill ride which gave them an opportunity to put on more speed.

Juniper's superior style soon told. Emma, on her more sedate mount, came along in Ross's wake, eyeing him with a deepening sense of resentment. There was something about his back, about the tilt of his head, that shouted triumph at her. He was enjoying himself.

He waited for her at the far end, watching her approach with a little smile on that well-cut mouth. Even at a distance she could not fail to catch the smug self-satisfaction in his eyes as they flickered over her.

She drew rein and eyed him back resentfully.

He grinned. 'Slow but steady does it!'

'Pleased with yourself, aren't you?'

Laughter filled his gaze. 'My, my, we are cross, aren't we?'

'I feel like ... like a ...' Words failed her. 'Trailing along behind you like that!'

'Like a squaw?' He was openly laughing now. It was maddening. 'Well, you could hardly ride my horse, could you? A tiny creature like you! You'd never hold him.'

'Oh, wouldn't I? Try me!' She was blazing now.

'Reckless girl,' he teased. 'Of course you couldn't. Your wrists aren't strong enough to hold him.'

'Get down and let me try,' she challenged.

His smile vanished. 'No,' he said firmly. 'Don't be absurd!' Turning Juniper he headed back towards the stables. Emma rode behind him in silence, rigid with irritation. In the yard he slid down and turned to greet Lucy, who came out in some surprise to greet them.

'You're back early——' she began, then broke off in astonishment as Emma, having dismounted from her quiet grey, snatched the reins from Ross's unwary hand, mounted Juniper and was off in a flash.

'My God,' Ross ground out in incredulous alarm. 'She's mad! That demon of a horse will half kill her!' He looked at Marcy and discounted her, raced into another stall and brought out a sinewy black horse which he mounted bareback. Ted ran out cursing and protesting

'Ross knows what he's doing,' Lucy dismissed as Ross and the black disappeared after Emma.

'I hope he does,' Ted growled, 'or he'll be a dead man! Dancer cannot abide a strange rider.' He shook his head ominously. 'He may ride pretty well, but he doesn't know all Dancer's wicked tricks. He's a death-trap on four legs, that horse!'

CHAPTER SEVEN

EMMA was already regretting her impulsive display. Her common sense told her that Juniper had been excited by her sudden switch of mounts. Horses sensed the emotions of their riders. The big bay's shoulders heaved nervously, his ears flicked back and forth, as he headed straight for the wood. When, deciding to return and eat the humble pie Ross would undoubtedly demand of her, Emma tried to turn his head and go back, the bay flung up his head with a shrill whinny and held fiercely to his course, ignoring her hands and knees, the command of her voice.

She tried again, with all her determination, but Juniper was immovable. He was under the trees now, his sweating coat dappled by autumn sunlight. His pace quickened, he turned off the sandy bridle path into the thicker tangle of trees and brushwood which wound deeper into the wood, the paths narrow and criss-crossed, becoming more like rabbit tracks than real paths. Birds flew up on all sides, making distinctive alarm calls. Juniper snorted and tossed his head, his muscles rippling under his glossy coat.

She tried again to calm him, leaning forward, her hand smoothing his flanks, whispering gently, with an air meant to reassure him and bring him back to himself.

'Good boy, Juniper ... good boy ...'

He plunged and fretted, trying to dislodge her. A man-high gorse bush sent thin needles of thorns into her calves. She winced and tried to move Juniper away, but he was desperate to throw her, to rid himself of this unwanted burden, and his plunging continued.

Suddenly she heard hooves thudding, hard and rhythmically on the sandy track, somewhere close by, and called as loudly as she could, hoping her voice would carry above the sound. She knew who it was—knew who it must be, and her heart contracted with pleasure and relief knowing that Ross was coming.

'Ross! Ross! Over here ...'

He had heard the sounds of Juniper before she called, and had turned off in pursuit of them. Emma heard the cracking of twigs, the snapping of branches, behind her, then a great black horse appeared, with Ross barely holding him, riding bareback, his thigh almost seemingly part of the great animal, which snorted and twisted yet was held in control by that invisible power of will which the man exerted.

Ross looked, indeed, at that moment, like an avenging fury; his dark brows drawn in a black bar above his eyes, his hair blown into wildness by the wind. He was white as he glared at her, his eyes like chips of granite, narrowed in rage.

'My God, you don't deserve to be alive! You stupid, damnable girl! When I think what could have happened ...' His teeth ground together as he swallowed the rest of the words.

'I'm sorry, Ross.' Her voice came faint and ashamed, but she met his furious gaze, head lifted, not in defiance but with self-disgust. She had risked her own life and that of the horse when she flung off in a temper just to show Ross that she was as good a rider as he was ... she had been showing off. It was indefensible.

'I should hope you were,' he said tightly.

He had Juniper's bridle now, his strong brown hand clenched on the leather. Juniper was quieter, calmed by Ross's very presence, aware that a new element had been called into play.

'Get down,' Ross told her crisply.

Emma obeyed, thankful to stand on firm ground once more, her legs somewhat shaky after her ordeal.

Ross turned Juniper's head, began to move off.

'Where are you going?' she called, not believing her eyes. He could not mean to abandon her here, surely?

'You can walk back,' he snapped. 'It may well teach you a well-deserved lesson.'

'Ross!'

He did not even look back. Leading the bay and riding the great black horse with straight-backed ease, he disappeared towards the sandy bridle track without a word.

'Ross!' Her voice rose angrily, sending the birds spiralling upwards again, uttering cries of irritation and alarm. 'Ross, wait for me!'

She followed him, along the trail of broken branches, crushed leaves, trodden bracken. The scent of sap and earth rose fresh and heady around her. She saw a grey squirrel scamper up an ash tree. A crow screamed hoarsely, amused and mocking. Ross was out of sight when she gained the bridle path. She heard hoofbeats in the distance, the two horses moving at a calm trot.

'Damn him,' Emma said softly, half amused, half furious. 'He might have waited!'

She hurried forward, then winced, remembering the thorns which Juniper had managed to embed in her legs. Looking down, she saw several thorns still projecting from her sturdy blue jeans. The material had deflected some, no doubt, but others had pierced right through the cloth.

She bent and pulled them out, wincing as she did so, and looking at the thorns with distaste. When she lifted her jeans and inspected her calves she found that her skin was scratched and bleeding in a number of places.

'I won't ride Juniper again,' she told herself. 'Ross was right about him!' Then she grimaced at the thought. There was nothing as maddening as a man who was always right!

She found her handkerchief, dabbed the blood away as best she could, then rolled down her jeans again and set off at a steady pace.

Ross met her at the edge of the wood. He stood,

hands in his pockets, watching her approach with a mocking tilt of the head. 'It's going to be a long walk home,' he said maliciously. 'Think you can make it?'

'I'll make it,' she said flatly.

His eyes narrowed. 'Are you limping?'

'No,' she lied, averting her gaze.

He caught her by the shoulder to halt her, knelt and rolled back the left leg of her jeans until the red, scratched shin came into view. The cuts were bleeding again. Ross swore under his breath.

'How the hell did you do this? They look like razor cuts.'

'Thorns,' she said succinctly.

'So Juniper did throw you?' He looked up at her, his hands absently moving as he wiped the blood away with his own handkerchief. 'Why didn't you tell me?'

'He didn't throw me,' she said. 'He just tried to —he kept plunging around near a huge gorse bush. My legs took the brunt of it.'

'It looks painful,' he said tightly. 'I hope it is. It may teach you a lesson. I'd like to beat you!' He rolled down her jeans, stood up and stared at her broodingly. 'Now how am I to get you home? You can't walk in that condition.'

'It isn't far,' she said. 'I'll manage.'

He shook his head. 'No. Hang on ... I've had an idea. Wait here ...' He ran back along the road. In a short time he was back, riding a rather ancient bicycle. He grinned at her. 'You can sit in front.'

'It looks very unsteady,' she said doubtfully. 'Are you sure it's roadworthy?'

'It will save your legs,' he said. 'Come on, girl, take a chance!'

Perched uncertainly in front of him, she shut her eyes as they freewheeled down Bundle Lane, the old machine rustily protesting at their combined weight. Air rushed past her face. Then sun warmed her skin, the wind blew back her hair against Ross's cheek. His arm held her tightly, his chest pressed against her shoulders.

'I borrowed this from Lucy Todd,' he said close to her ear.

'I hope you didn't tell her anything too alarming,' she said. 'It was really my fault, not Juniper's, you know. I frightened him.'

'I told her the truth. Considering how many kinds of danger you were risking, a few thorns were a very mild punishment.' His voice was penetrating. 'You brought this on yourself.'

'I've admitted it,' she said tautly.

'So I should let bygones be bygones?' His tones were scathing.

'I won't do anything so foolish again,' she said, then with a return of her fiery irritation against him she added, 'But you might try being less aggravating yourself! You have a lordly manner which is enough to make the mildest female rise in rebellion!'

'And you certainly aren't the mildest female,' he retorted with undisguised amusement.

'You know very well you drove me to do it! You were far too cocksure!'

He laughed softly, and his hands tightened on her waist. Emma looked down at them, strong brown hands, hard and firm, with deft fingers which were capable of so much. Then she shrieked, 'You aren't steering!'

One hand moved away, lazily adjusted the handle-bars as they spun crazily towards the hedge. They veered back into line once more and the cottage came into view.

'Home sweet home,' said Ross contentedly.

'I'm longing for a bath,' Emma groaned. 'Every muscle of me is aching ...'

'Good!' Ross was infuriatingly amused.

The old machine slowed down as they turned a last, hedge-blind corner, and then Ross spun into a final spurt, only to draw a deep breath of which Emma was immediately, painfully conscious, as they came in sight of the sleek car drawn up on the grassy edge of the road outside the cottage gate.

Emma knew it at once, before she saw the chauffeur in his peaked cap and dark uniform.

Ross's hand tightened again on her wrist, yet this time she knew no personal pleasure in the intimacy of the touch. Ross's mind was not on her, she sensed.

He braked carefully before they reached the car. 'You'd better run down to Mrs Pat's and get the children,' he said quietly.

'Yes,' she said, forgetting her desire to have a bath, the pain of her scratched legs. Was this the long-awaited reconciliation? Had the old financier come at last to see his grandchildren?

She slid down while Ross steadied the bicycle and walked past the car towards the whitewashed inn at the end of the lane. She kept her eyes averted from the back of the car. She did not want to know if Leon Daumaury was alone, or if he had brought a triumphant, taunting-eyed Amanda with him to witness the family reunion. Ross had made it clear that she, Emma, had no part in this moment. She had been sent to fetch the children, her role as children's nanny firmly re-established for the benefit of Amanda, no doubt.

Back straight, eyes clear, Emma had no intention of permitting herself any weakness. She found the three children cosily seated around the fire with Mrs Pat, reading a tatty, dogeared edition of Beatrix Potter.

Edie was ironing, her cheeks pink, her eyes contented. Mrs Pat looked up as Emma came into the kitchen, and grinned at her.

'You're back early, m'dear.'

'We have visitors,' Emma said.

Her tone was careful, but Mrs Pat looked shrewdly back at her and lifted one eyebrow.

'Have you, then? My, my.' She looked at the three children. 'You need a bit of a wash and brush up before you go home, m'dears. Edie . . .'

Edie obligingly led them away, protesting. Mrs Pat smiled at Emma, observing the storm signals in her face, the suspicious over-brightness of the brown eyes.

'Visitors, you say?' she probed gently.

'Leon Daumaury, I think,' Emma said flatly.

'Ah,' said Mrs Pat on a long, indrawn breath. She rose and poured Emma a cup of tea from the fat brown pot which never seemed to be empty. 'You look as if you need this!'

Emma drank thirstily, smiled at her. 'I did. Thank you. Life is rather like a switchback, isn't it? Just as you're going along nicely you get flung off into outer space again.'

'Maybe we get too complacent if life is too easy,' Mrs Pat said. 'Folk can get awful smug.'

Emma laughed. 'I'm surprised they ever get the chance. I'm in a constant state of surprise.'

'An exciting life,' Mrs Pat said, amused.

'You're making fun of me,' said Emma, unwillingly forced to smile.

'Me? Never,' said Mrs Pat unconvincingly. She looked round as Edie appeared once more with the children, their faces pink and clean. 'Spick and span? That's right. Off you go with your Emma, then.' She sighed. 'Lucky you had an early lunch.'

'I wish I had,' Emma said, feeling ravenous. Her adventures in Boxrey Wood had given her an appetite, and even the pain of Ross walking towards Amanda again had not taken the edge off her hunger. 'I'm a boringly down-to-earth female,' she said to Mrs Pat. 'Nothing has ever deprived me of my appetite for long. You'll never find me pining away, I'm afraid. I'm too disgustingly healthy.'

'And a good thing, too,' said Mrs Pat. 'Edie shall take the children back. You stay here and eat some lunch.'

Emma hesitated. It was tempting. She would not, then, have to see Ross and Amanda together; to witness a family reunion in which she had no part whatever, to feel shut out and alien to the new happiness around her. And anyway, Leon Daumaury, whatever his faults, had a right to privacy in these precious moments with his grandchildren. He would not want an observer to be present.

'That's very kind of you,' she said doubtfully. 'Thank you, I'd like that.'

'Sit down, then,' Mrs Pat said, nodding at Edie, who quietly led the children away. Tracy looked back, dark-browed, looking rather alarmed, some sort of intuition springing into her mind.

'Visitors? What visitors, Emma?'

'Come along,' Edie said gently.

When they had gone Mrs Pat made Emma a herb omelette, golden and creamy inside, with a crisp, white-fleshed apple to follow, and cheese available if she wanted some. 'I like cheese with an apple,' Mrs Pat said, pouring her a cup of coffee.

Emma drank her coffee by the fire, reluctant to move, then thanked Mrs Pat and made a slow return to the cottage. The car had gone, she was relieved to see, and when she came into the kitchen she found Edie and the children alone, busy making fairy cakes for tea.

'Ross has been called out to Duckett's Farm,' Tracy told her casually, preparing the cake trays.

'Oh?' Emma tried to look indifferent.

Robin looked round at her, his bright eyes curious. 'There weren't any visitors, Emma.'

Tracy and he stared at her, waiting for her reply. Emma was taken aback. Had something gone wrong? Had Leon Daumaury altered his mind? Or had he, perhaps, never been in the sleek limousine? Had it been Amanda by herself?

'I must have been mistaken, then,' she said lamely.

'It was Amanda, I suppose,' Tracy said in disgust. 'I'm glad she'd gone by the time we got here.'

'So'm I,' Robin agreed wholeheartedly.

'Mm ...' Donna added with such fervour that they all laughed. Then Emma said quietly, 'You mustn't say things like that about Amanda, children.'

'Why not?' asked Robin, the acute.

'Because you must not be rude about grown-ups,' Emma said in a certain confusion. She might have more truthfully said that they might one day find themselves with Amanda for an aunt, and they would have to put up with it.

'You aren't working,' Edie said reproachfully at that moment, and the three children turned back to the work in hand.

Emma spent half an hour writing to Fanny, filling in the details of what had happened to her since she left London, making it all sound gay and amusing, she hoped, and dwelling carefully on a long description of the three children. Fanny would be worried about her, no doubt, and this would ease her mind. She posted it and then returned for tea, after which she played dominoes with the three children, allowing Donna to share her hand so that she felt she was really taking part.

Ross did not return until much later. The children were all in bed. Edie was knitting a bright yellow sweater for Robin. Emma was working on some sketches, her face smoothly absorbed.

She looked up, sensing his presence. He was watching her oddly, his face enigmatic. As her eyes met his, she felt his gaze probing her expression, as if seeking some answer to an unspoken question.

Half resentful, half wary, she lifted her brows. 'Something wrong? You look grim.'

His face relaxed, as if he had found the answer to whatever was troubling him. He grinned casually.

'Nothing wrong. Do I look grim? You look like a little girl ready for bed.'

She had had her belated bath, put on pyjamas and dressing-gown afterwards, her gleaming chestnut hair damp and curling back from her pink face, tied with an old pink ribbon.

'Do you want something to eat?' she asked, putting away her work. 'Was it Mr Duckett's cow again?'

He laughed. 'Not this time. Mrs Duckett's pet spaniel—he'd got his paw trapped in a grating.'

'Oh, poor thing. What did you do?' Emma's quick sympathies were aroused.

'What they should have done before calling me ... soaped his paw. It slid out easily then.'

She laughed. 'Of course!' Then she shot him a guarded look. 'But you've been gone hours ...' Then she bit her lip, wishing she could recall the remark. She did not want him to think she counted the minutes while he was away. He must never guess how she felt about him.

'I went into Dorchester to see Edward,' he said easily. 'We had to go over the accounts. It's a long and tedious job.'

'How is Chloe? I really liked her,' said Emma, with enthusiasm. 'She's such a warm, kind person. It was fun just being with her.'

He nodded. 'Chloe's fine. She likes you, too, by the way—she asked after you, said more or less what you've just said.' He looked at her with a faint smile. 'You're two of a kind—born home-makers.'

Emma flushed. The compliment was too sweet, too unexpected, for her to be able to bear it with equanimity. She looked away, beginning to tremble.

There was a little silence. She peeped at Ross and found him watching her, leaning carelessly against the door frame, his hands in his pockets and a wry expression on his face. An expression which seemed to say ... well, what have I said? Ross probably found her obvious embarrassment very embarrassing! Didn't she know, hadn't he told her a hundred times already that he did not want to get involved with females? That he steered clear of such involvement like the plague?

She went into the kitchen, back very straight, eyes guarded. 'I'll make your coffee,' she said.

'I thought you said a meal?' He followed her.

'If you were at Chloe's house you've had a meal,' she said firmly. 'Chloe never let anyone leave without feeding them to the brim!'

He laughed. 'Isn't that the truth? She loves to see people eat, especially men. It must be some sort of tribal custom.'

'She's hospitable,' said Emma in a squashing tone. 'Don't you make fun of Chloe!'

'I wouldn't dare!' Ross gave a mock-shiver. 'I'd be too scared of that look in your beautiful big brown eyes!'

She made coffee, poured him a cup, without saying another word. Because he had said she was like Chloe she peculiarly took a great dislike to the mockery with which he had just alluded to her. If he made fun of Chloe he made fun of herself ...

He sat and drank his coffee in an easy chair before the fire. Emma pretended to go on with her sketching, concentrating without really seeing what her pencil was doing. Her mind was buzzing with questions she dared not ask him. How could she betray her curiosity? He would never forgive her, she knew him well enough to know that.

But how could she help wondering about that curtailed visit? *Who* had been in that car? She wished now, wished bitterly, that she had not been such a coward, that she had looked in the back, seen whatever was to be seen, even if it was, as she had feared, Amanda's mocking, malicious, triumphant smile.

All this feuding business was so silly, so wrong, that she had to hope that Leon Daumaury would forgive his son and daughter-in-law, take back the family into loving relationship, welcome his grandchildren. It was right and proper that he should do so, and Emma was sad to know that he still held off aloof from them. How could anyone, let alone a grandfather, reject little Donna, Robin and proud little Tracy?

Why had Ross sent her to fetch the children if it had not been their grandfather who had come to visit them? Or had he only been getting rid of her, Emma, so that he could talk to Amanda alone?

She winced inwardly. That was a possibility. It made sense of the peculiar little incident—painful sense. She squared her shoulders. She would face it, painful or no. What else was there to do, anyway?

I'm beginning to make a habit of it, she told herself with fierce self-contempt; a habit of facing unpalatable thoughts, of admitting unpleasant facts. It was a wearing way of life. Why do I fall in love with the wrong men? she asked herself angrily. Why don't I grow up, learn some sense?

She went to bed early, eager to forget pain in oblivion, and slept deeply, her dreams troubled and shifting.

She woke to a cool, cloudy morning. The wind had changed during the night. There was a scent of rain in the air.

Ross went off early. Edie went down to the inn to work with her sister, and Emma, having done what needed to be done about the house, decided to take the children for a walk.

The gorse was sparkling with spiders' webs of all shapes and varieties. There had been a heavy dew the night before, and the leaves were still damp and glistening. The damp earth gave off a leaf-mould odour, rather reminiscent of graveyards, and there were pale fungi growing on the sides of the trees.

They walked casually, halting now and then to inspect some particularly interesting object Robin had found—a scarlet spray of berries, an enormous acorn still wearing its beige cup-hat, a patch of bright emerald moss making a fairy cushion under a great beech tree.

Emma had brought paper and pencils so that they could all do some sketching. Donna drew a holly bush, all huge berries and thin angular leaves. Robin drew a beech with huge snaky roots. Tracy did a far more careful, more realistic sketch of a woodland glade, with a squirrel thrown in for good measure, drawn from memory rather than sight.

Tracy, of course, was scathing on the subject of Donna's holly and Robin's tree. 'They don't look like that,' she commented. 'You can't draw for toffee!'

A squabble developed, naturally, which was only settled by Emma, hurriedly intervening to suggest that they stop drawing and have a little race down to the wide path to the cart track which ran through the fields and ended at the back of the inn.

'We always go that way,' complained Tracy. 'Let's go the other way.'

'Yes,' the others agreed, 'let's!'

Emma, to keep the peace, agreed, and they walked another way along narrow, hedged lanes, stopping to talk to some sheep over a gate. The sheep stared back, mild-eyed, incurious, their long narrow faces blank.

'Silly old sheep,' Robin said, disgusted.

'They're terribly stupid, poor things,' Tracy agreed.

'Baa baa,' Donna said happily, undeterred by the lack of response.

'Oh, come on,' said Tracy, kicking a flat white stone along the road. Robin and she raced off, playing a game of football with the stone, leaving Emma and Donna to bring up the rear.

Children were very tiring, Emma thought wearily. They needed such unflagging attention! She held Donna's hand tightly and fitted her own long stride to Donna's cheerful trot.

She had done so little of her own work since coming down here. She really must get something of this Hardy stuff done! She had intended to work in the evenings, but somehow she was always so tired after a day with the children.

The lane ended suddenly, at a mysterious gate, shaped like a horseshoe, made of green-painted wood and set in a red-brick wall.

'I never saw that before,' said Tracy dubiously. 'I wonder where we are?'

'We've come the wrong way, I'm afraid,' Emma said, suddenly suspecting that this was the wall surrounding Queen's Daumaury. 'We'd better go back.'

'It's the gate to a magic land,' said Robin dreamily, staring up at the gleaming brass door knob which served as a handle. 'Oh, let's go inside, Emma.'

'Certainly not. It's private,' Emma said, uneasy and alarmed.

Tracy stared at her. 'Come on,' she said sharply, turning away. Had she, too, guessed where the mysterious gate led?

Robin stood, obstinate and entranced, staring upwards. Tracy grabbed his arm, then froze, as there was a grating sound and the green gate began to move inwards. The three children stood, staring, as the gate opened, as if expecting to see a fairy, or a wizard in weird robes, framed in the doorway.

Emma knew, with fatalistic dismay, whom they would see. Fate had led them here, at this moment of time, just as their grandfather, leaning on a gold-mounted cane, came stepping through the green gate and stopped, thunderous, to stare at them in disbelief.

CHAPTER EIGHT

AFTER a long silence he spoke in a thready voice. 'What does this mean?' He looked at Emma as he spoke, expecting her to reply, and his eyes were angry. Frail though he was he exuded power and certainty of command. Emma was shaken by his appearance, by his presence.

Before she could speak, however, Tracy had spoken, her voice clear and scornful.

'We're just going. We came here by mistake. We didn't know you lived here or we wouldn't have come!'

'Tracy!' Emma spoke sharply, shocked by the child's bluntness. She looked at Mr Daumaury. 'I'm sorry, that was very rude of her.'

He was staring down at Tracy, his brows together. 'You have a sharp tongue, miss.'

Tracy stared back at him, mulishly silent.

'Are you my grandfather?' Robin asked, in his patient but unshakeable fashion.

Leon Daumaury looked at him, and something passed over his old face, a flicker which he quickly eradicated. After a pause he said flatly, 'Yes, I am.'

'Do you live in there?' Robin peered through the

green gate into the rolling vista of parkland. 'Where's your house?'

'Would you like to see it?' Leon Daumaury asked him, his eyes fixed on the child's face.

Robin lifted excited eyes. 'Yes, I would. It must be very small and round, like an elf house ...'

The old eyes widened, as if Leon Daumaury had had a shock. 'An elf house? Small and ...' He sounded almost as if he were breathless. He looked at Emma, searching her face with his fierce hawk-like eyes. 'What does the child mean? Surely he knows ...?'

'He knows nothing, I imagine,' Emma said gently.

The old man winced. 'Nothing?' He looked through the green gate. 'Nothing of Queen's Daumaury?'

Emma nodded.

Leon Daumaury held out a frail, gnarled hand towards Robin, and the boy confidently slid his own tiny fingers into the old ones.

'We'll go and see, shall we?' Leon Daumaury looked at Emma over Robin's head. 'Will you bring the others, Miss ...?'

'I'm Emma Leigh,' she said.

'Their nurse, I understand?' His fierce eyes were penetrating, shrewd.

'Yes,' she said flatly.

'I don't think we ought to go,' Tracy said suddenly. 'Mummy wouldn't like it.'

Emma hesitated, uncertain and troubled. Tracy might well be right. She did not know what to do. It was not really her decision, was it? She ought to let Ross decide. But what was she to say to this old man who held Robin's hand so tightly?

'I think, perhaps, Tracy is right,' she said haltingly. 'I'm sorry ...'

'Tracy doesn't know what Mummy likes,' Robin said in his most adult, careful tone. 'She guesses— and usually she's wrong.' He looked at Emma seriously. 'Like she was about porridge and Donna. Tracy's bossy, awfully bossy.'

Donna was staring into the parkland, her face suddenly full of shining excitement. 'I see something ... what that?' Her words slid together in her eagerness to communicate, but Emma understood the drift of what she meant.

A hundred yards away, beyond a clump of bushes, a young roe deer grazed peacefully.

'A doe,' Leon Daumaury told Donna gruffly.

Donna's smooth brow wrinkled. She lifted puzzled, doubtful eyes to his face. 'A doe?'

'A female deer,' he told her, clearing his throat. 'You're very like your mother, my dear.'

Donna giggled. So did Robin. Their grandfather looked at them in half-offended astonishment. 'What's funny?' he demanded.

'You called Donna my dear,' Robin said. 'That's a deer, and Donna's a dear ...' He and Donna giggled explosively. Tracy looked at them in silent disapproval, her face as stony as a monument.

Mr Daumaury smiled, his face transformed as if by a miracle into a warm and living countenance, all his coldness and remoteness falling away.

"The English language is very strange, isn't it, my

140

dears?' He emphasised the word and was delighted by their immediate response.

They shrieked with laughter, and Robin began to run forward, dragging the old man after him, while Donna toddled along beside them. Emma looked helplessly at Tracy who was staring at this scene in icy disgust.

'I think we shall have to accept a fait accompli,' Emma said gently.

Tracy set her lower lip in mutinous rejection. 'I'm going home!'

Emma caught her arm. 'You can't! Not alone, Tracy. I'm afraid you must come with us. I can't allow you to go wandering off alone, you know that.'

'Mummy doesn't like our grandfather,' Tracy repeated.

'I don't think you're old enough to be certain what your mother likes or does not like,' Emma said very carefully. 'You may think you know, darling, but grown-ups sometimes don't even know themselves. Things are often more complicated than they seem on the surface. I think we should let Robin and Donna talk to Mr Daumaury if they want to—I'll explain to your mummy when I see her.'

'She'll be furious with you,' Tracy said with undisguised triumph.

'Oh, Tracy,' sighed Emma, 'why are you so difficult?' Was it because Tracy was the oldest? Did she feel the pressure of her younger brother and sister, did she feel the need to assert herself whenever she could?

Emma looked down at the pale, set little face and was suddenly filled with pity and affection for the child. She knelt and held her, pressing her close, her lips touching Tracy's cold cheek. 'Don't look like that,' she whispered.

Tracy suffered the indignity for a moment, then broke free and ran off into the park calling to Robin wait for her. Emma felt the pain of rejection for a moment, then she smiled and stood up. After all, Tracy had changed her mind, hadn't she? She had joined the others instead of sulking here alone. Some sort of contact had been made.

Walking behind the little quartet, Emma thought with some amusement of the enormous education she was receiving from these children. She was supposed to be in charge of them, to be guiding and teaching them—she was supposed to be the clever adult. Yet she knew that she had learnt far more than she had taught. Tracy, Robin and Donna had opened her eyes to many hitherto unnoticed facets of human feeling and thinking. She was much the wiser for having known them. Each day she learnt something new. They were so fascinating, so complex, so enchanting, so maddening.

Is this how mothers feel? she wondered. When they're not completely baffled, exhausted and drained of all their energies?

Perhaps it was because one had to concentrate on another human being for so many hours, watch and anticipate its needs, its griefs, its nature. Usually one only observed oneself with that sort of depth, and one learned little from such internal scrutiny.

Watching children revealed much about human nature in the raw.

Through the landscaped vistas of the park they wandered while Leon Daumaury explained, showed and boasted of its marvels. He pointed out a silver pheasant, pale ghostly birds which shyly hid as they passed, their muted plumage making it hard to see them when they hid in shadow, although they were so large, stately as dowagers when they walked through the long grass. Robin was not enthusiastic.

'I like the pheasants we see in the fields better than them,' he said simply. 'They're a jolly colour, brown and fat—like Mrs Pat's teapot. Or,' he added thoughtfully, glancing sideways at her, 'like Emma.'

Emma laughed. So did Leon Daumaury, on an astonished bark. 'I hardly think your Emma is fat,' he added, though. 'She does have something of the colouring of a male pheasant, I grant you. Who is Mrs Pat, though?'

'Don't you know Mrs Pat? She knows you,' said Robin.

'And Edie,' Donna added loyally, nodding like a wise little Mandarin.

'Edie?' The old man looked down at Donna, smiling encouragingly. 'Tell me about Edie and Mrs Pat. They sound very interesting.'

'I love them,' said Donna, and the words encompassed volumes. Leon Daumaury looked a little taken aback, as if suddenly shown a glimpse of something he had not suspected existed.

'They run the inn in the village,' Emma said swiftly.

'Oh, those people,' Mr Daumaury said, in astonishment. 'Well, of course, I've seen them—from a distance.'

'They've seen you, too,' Robin encouraged kindly.

The old man was watching Donna's small face with wonder. 'Why do you love them?' he asked her abruptly.

She lifted wide eyes. 'I do,' she said, baffled by her lack of the necessary words. She could not explain—she could state the fact, that was all. His question worried her, she frowned.

Emma slipped a hand over the tiny fingers which curled and clung to hers at once. Quietly she said, 'Donna loves Edie and Mrs Pat because they love her. They're kind and loving people, both of them.'

'So,' said Leon Daumaury with a faint trace of disdain and a wry amusement, 'my silver pheasants are too grand for you three, are they? You prefer the common or garden pheasants you see every day?'

'Common or field pheasants,' said Robin.

His grandfather laughed again, that sharp, surprised bark of a sound. He looked at the boy with respect, then he looked at Emma. 'Sharp as a needle, this one,' he murmured.

'Where are the flowers?' Donna asked Emma.

'The gardens are nearer the house,' said Leon Daumaury himself in reply.

They were walking along a wide path through open parkland, elegantly laid out by some genius of a landscape artist so that wherever the eye rested it fell upon some charming scene—a clump of rhododendrons, an oak tree, a silver birch. Suddenly the path twisted to the right and there, through the trees, they saw the house, surprisingly close to them.

It was well deserving of its fame, an almost perfect specimen of its kind; exquisitely proportioned, built of creamy stone, with a portico over the front door, a row of flat, elegant windows and that air of being in good taste which was somehow typical of the eighteenth century.

Robin stood and stared at it while his grandfather watched his face almost hungrily, his wrinkled features intent upon the boy and aware of nothing else.

'Well?' he demanded when Robin remained silent.

Robin lifted his clear, alarmingly adult eyes to him. 'I wish I lived in your house,' he said bluntly.

Leon Daumaury's skin slowly flushed, his lower lip trembled, and he closed his lips together in an effort to stem the emotion Emma could read in his face. After a moment he said gruffly, 'I'm glad you like it.'

They walked slowly round to the back of the house. A terrace ran along here, the wooden columns supporting a glass roof, and roses spilled everywhere in waves of scent and colour, despite the lateness of the season. 'In summer they're the talk of the county,' Leon Daumaury told Emma, seeing her eyes rest on the roses. 'We're proud of our roses at Queen's Daumaury.'

'What's that?' asked Donna in dismay, shrinking back at a sudden raucous shriek.

'Peacocks,' said Tracy abruptly.

Her grandfather looked at her, his eyes keen. 'D'you like them?'

'They show off,' Tracy said scornfully. 'All those feathers ...'

'Oh, pretty,' Donna cried, seeing a cock spread his tail feathers in glittering panoply. 'Oh, pretty!'

They all stood, in satisfied silence, admiring the spread of colour. 'There's no denying it,' Emma said with a laugh, 'they are fantastic creatures, aren't they?' She looked at Tracy and smiled. 'I sympathise with your point of view, darling, but one has to admire them!'

'I suppose they're very pretty,' Tracy reluctantly admitted.

'You wait until you see the gardens in the spring,' said Leon Daumaury. 'We have a blue garden here —in the spring it's a sea of blue hyacinth, then later forget-me-not and love-in-a-mist, larkspur and iris ... it's quite breathtaking.'

'I love blue flowers,' said Tracy, on an involuntary surge of enthusiasm.

'There's a wild garden, too,' the old man added. 'We call it the Coppice—there are hazel trees, a little stream and glades filled with bluebells and wood anemones in the spring, with cowslips and ladies' slippers and a dozen different varieties later. The gardeners leave it alone to encourage wild flowers to seed there—the birds carry the seeds in their beaks, you know, and some blow in on the wind.'

'Dandelion clocks,' said Tracy knowingly.

'Yes,' he nodded.

Donna was standing at a french window, her nose pressed against the glass. 'Can we go in?' she asked her grandfather.

Before he could answer a window was flung open above Donna and Amanda cried in sharp, angry tones, 'What are you doing here? Go away at once, you naughty child!'

Leon Daumaury stepped forward. He had been hidden from Amanda's sight until he moved. Now she stared, going pale, having thought that Donna was alone.

'Oh, I didn't see ... I didn't know ...'

Sternly the old man said, 'You shouldn't have shouted at the child like that. You've frightened her.'

Donna was not frightened, merely startled. Emma knew her well enough to recognise the look of mild contentment which now crept into the big blue eyes. Donna was enjoying this—she did not like Amanda and was glad to see her getting into trouble, particularly as Amanda had just made her jump in alarm.

Amanda bit her lip and tried to appear contrite. 'I didn't recognise her. I just saw a strange child on the terrace, peering in the window, and I thought ...'

'Considering her obvious age you shouldn't have shouted, whatever she was doing—she's only a baby,' Leon Daumaury said coldly.

Amanda flung Emma a look of bitter hatred. Emma knew whom Amanda blamed for this incident. Then, with a flicker of her lashes, the other girl smiled at the three children. 'Oh, they know me, don't you? We're old friends now. We understand each other.'

'We certainly do,' said Robin in a hilarious imitation of Ross.

His grandfather looked at him sharply. Emma wondered if he knew Ross, and perhaps recognised the turn of phrase, the tone. Of course, she thought —Ross had visited the house now and then to see Amanda. Leon Daumaury must know him, even if he detested Ross's sister for having married his son.

Amanda opened the french windows and they all entered the room beyond. It was one of those much photographed for glossy magazines. A drawing-room in shades of pale blue and creamy beige—the walls papered with a silky sandy material, the carpet a tone poem in blue and cream, the furniture upholstered in blue brocade. Blue vases stood on occasional tables, containing exquisitely arranged flowers, dahlias in warm autumn shades which looked discreetly colourful against the muted elegance of the walls.

The children looked out of place in here. Their humanity, their zest, was not in accord with the atmosphere of this monument to good taste.

Robin and Tracy exchanged silent glances. Donna moved nearer to Emma and clutched her hand tightly.

Leon Daumaury looked down at their expressive faces, and gave a very wry little smile. 'I'll take you to see the rest of the house quickly,' he said.

It was all much the same—a house meant for adults leading elegant adult lives. The furniture was frail, highly polished, beautiful. Every finger-mark would show at once. Tables and chairs were dainty, thin-legged, finely balanced. The children shrank from them instinctively.

'You don't like it,' said their grandfather flatly.

'Is there a room for children?' asked Robin with an effort at politeness.

Leon Daumaury smiled that wry smile. 'The nurseries? On the top floor. The attics, now. They haven't been used since ...' He broke off.

Since his son was a child? thought Emma. She wondered about the children's father—was he an archaeologist because his life in this elegant box of a house had made him the sort of man who can patiently dis-inter ancient lives?

They mounted to the top of the house. On this floor the carpets vanished. The floorboards were varnished a dark brown, polished and shiny. The doors were varnished, too, and the only light came from a skylight in the roof.

They opened the door and the children went forward slowly into a long, narrow room with strange, uneven ceilings, many odd corners and sloping walls.

'Oh!' breathed Robin in delight, then he ran forward. In the middle of the room, on a very worn piece of carpet, stood an old rocking horse, his mane thinned out by clasping hands, his colours dim and faded but his eyes as bright as ever.

Robin was on his back in a flash. Donna cried, 'Me too!'

Emma lifted her on to the horse, and she clutched Robin round the waist while he ecstatically rocked away. Tracy gazed round the room, staring at the bookshelves loaded with well-read children's books, the toy cupboard left open so that a dogeared teddy bear peered out at them, the table and chairs, the quaint old nursery pictures of lambs with ribbons round their necks and little girls in summery hats.

She went to the window and looked out over the park. Emma heard her sigh. 'It's nice up here. The nicest place we've seen.'

Leon Daumaury watched them in silence. Emma suspected that he was moved to tears, but the light was fast fading and she could not be sure.

'It's raining,' Tracy said suddenly. 'How dark it's getting! Is it a storm, Emma?'

Emma anxiously joined her. The sky was black and clouded. 'I'm afraid it does look very stormy. We must hurry back to our lunch.'

'Have it here,' Leon Daumaury said gruffly.

Emma shook her head. 'Thank you, but no. It's ready for us at the cottage.'

She had popped it into the oven before they left— a nice warming casserole. It would be spoiled if they did not go back soon.

Robin was reluctant to part with his new friend the rocking horse. He gave him a last loving pat as he was borne away. Donna cried, too, and was cross with Emma for a few moments before she forgot all about it.

'I'll send you back in the car,' the old man said as they made their way down the shining staircase to the marble-floored hall.

'Thank you,' said Emma. She would have preferred to walk, but it would take too long. They would have to get back quickly.

Mr Daumaury stood on the steps, waving to them, as the car drew away. The children waved back as long as he was in their view, then leaned back to enjoy the luxury of the sleek, purring limousine.

'A great car, isn't it?' Robin commented to Emma.

She smiled and nodded.

'I don't like that house,' Tracy said in her flattest, most disapproving voice.

Robin looked at her, his rosy round cheeks and bright eyes a contrast to her pale face. 'You're only saying that because you think Mummy will be cross we went there,' he said, with his customary shrewdness.

'I'm not, clever,' Tracy snapped.

'I want a big horse too,' Donna commented softly, snuggling up to Emma. 'A horse that rocks backwards and forwards.' To emphasise her point she began to rock vigorously, her thumb in her mouth like the stopper in a bottle.

'Yes, I liked the rocking horse too,' Robin agreed with quiet enthusiasm.

'Uncle Ross will be cross,' Tracy said.

'Why should he?' Robin demanded scornfully.

'If Mummy had wanted us to go to see our grand-

151

father, Uncle Ross would have taken us there,' Tracy replied.

Emma felt a pang of bitter alarm at the words. Tracy was unanswerably right. Ross would have done so, of course.

Ross was at the cottage when they arrived. He came slowly down to the gate as they climbed out of the limousine. Emma saw his unreadable face, the eyes watching without giving anything away, and her heart sank. Was he going to be angry? She began to marshal her arguments hurriedly—she had not intended to visit the house, it had been a chain of unforeseeable accidents which had led them there and brought them into contact with old Mr Daumaury.

Robin walked up to his uncle calmly, like an early Christian facing the lions.

'Hallo, Uncle Ross. We've been to see our grandfather,' he said in his direct manner. 'I like him.'

Ross looked down at his nephew thoughtfully, then up at Emma, eyes narrowed. 'So? Have you, indeed? How did that come to happen, I wonder?'

She began to explain hastily, stammering, 'We went f-f-for a walk, you see, and we found ourselves in a lane we'd never seen before, and there was ...'

'A little fairy gate,' Donna offered sweetly, sliding her hand into her uncle's and smiling beatifically at him. 'And out came our grandfather and we went to see his house, but it was too big. Then we saw where his rocky horse lived and we liked that ...'

'Rocking horse,' Tracy corrected.

'A big rocking horse,' Robin breathed ecstatic-ally. 'Donna and me galloped on it.'

Ross looked at Emma, neither frowning nor smiling, his face oddly blank. 'You have had a busy day, haven't you?' he murmured to the children.

Lunch was a subdued affair. The children were tired, and having eaten, went off to rest upstairs, with books to look at and orders to try to take a nap for an hour if they could. Tracy was a little contemptuous at this—she was too old for such baby treatment, she implied, but Robin and Donna did not argue. They were yawning and pale, ready for a little sleep.

Ross helped Emma with the washing up in silence at first, but she was under no illusions. She could feel the tension under his skin as he moved about. Sooner or later he would say what was in his thoughts.

It came at last, in a quiet question. 'Don't you think you should have been more discreet in what you knew, I imagine, to be a delicate situation?'

'I know nothing,' she said. 'I've been told nothing. I had to follow my instincts.'

'And what did they tell you?' He was scornful.

'They told me to bring the children home at once, and I would have done so had Donna not run off before I could catch her—it was out of my hands before I could decide how to tactfully get away.' She was suddenly angry. She had been deliberately left in the dark, yet he was blaming her for something she had been unable to avoid. 'It was an impossible situation in which I found myself, anyway. How could I be rude to Mr Daumaury? I didn't know what to do, what to say.'

'Amanda tells me——' he began, and then her temper flared.

'Amanda! She rang to warn you, I presume? She was furious to see the children there, of course. She detests them.'

'Be quiet!' Ross commanded, in a tone so quelling that her own voice froze in her throat and she began to shake slightly.

After a slight pause, he said less formidably, 'I think you're being less than fair to Amanda. Far from detesting the children, she's been working eagerly to re-establish relations between them and their grandfather. Amanda desires nothing more than to see the family together again.'

Emma bit her lip and did not reply. What could she say? Her own experience of Amanda had certainly been less than happy. The other girl had always been cruel-tongued, hostile and malicious towards her, and, so far, she had not shown much more pleasant behaviour towards the three children. Emma remembered that first meeting—the splash of green mould on Amanda's lovely clothes, the other girl's furious reaction, her vicious reaction towards Robin particularly—and she wondered if Ross knew Amanda at all.

She looked at him sideways. He was looking concerned, anxious. Was he wondering how he was to explain this to his sister?

'Of course,' she said, 'I take full responsibility. I'll tell Judith it was my fault.'

He laughed oddly. 'Silly girl! Be quiet, Emma. Be quiet.' Flinging down the tea towel, he walked out of the room. She watched him go with burning indignation beneath which ran pain, love, weariness.

It hurt that he should speak to her in that dismissive voice. A silly girl—that was how he saw her. That's what I am, she thought. Silly ... A fool to fall in love with this tough, arrogant man who was too blind to see the traps laid for him by a girl like Amanda. He had boasted that he would not make a mistake about love, that he saw Amanda clearly—yet by his own words just now he was obviously completely fooled by her. Or else Emma had mistaken what she saw and heard.

She frowned out of the window at the afternoon sky, windblown and storm-driven. Rain blew fiercely against the glass, clouding her view. Or was it her own tears blinding her as she wept silently, her hands gripping the kitchen sink, her cheeks as wet as the windowpane?

CHAPTER NINE

Two days later Emma was working in the garden with the children when she heard a car pulling up outside the gate. She straightened, a hand to her aching back, somewhat surprised, but imagining that Ross had finished early and come home for tea. He had said when he went out that he would not be back until later, but in his job he never quite knew when he would be free and when he would be working all the hours God sent. For the last forty-eight hours, in fact, he had been unusually busy, and they had seen little of him. It was possible that Edward had arranged for Ross to have a few hours' much-needed break.

The gate clicked and she gave an astonished gasp. Facing her, shy yet bravely determined, stood Fanny.

They both laughed, then flung themselves at one another, hugging and kissing with almost tearful emotion.

'What on earth are you doing here?' demanded Emma, when she had stood back to survey her friend. 'That's a nice suit. New?'

Fanny looked down at it with contentment. 'Yes,

first time of wearing, in fact. I'm glad you like it.' It was a pale blue woollen suit, figure-hugging but warm, in a classical, timeless design. Blue had always suited Fanny. She looked radiant, Emma noted with pleasure. Obviously love was being kind to her.

'How's Guy?' she asked without self-consciousness. Her love for Ross, she found, had freed her even of feeling shy about Guy.

Fanny beamed, 'Here's Guy to answer for himself.' She gestured behind Emma, who turned in surprise, laughing, and found herself face to face with him.

He kissed Emma so warmly on the cheek, his face all smiles, that Emma was astonished to remember that she had ever suspected he loved her. Guy's complete indifference could not be more obvious now that the scales had fallen from her eyes. He was the same cheerful, easy companion he had always been —it had been her mistake to imagine otherwise.

How we fool ourselves! she thought wryly. We imagine so much that's not true and miss the truth which is all around us!

'You both look so well!' It was true. They looked on top of the world.

Smiling, blushing, Fanny said, 'We came down to ask you to come back to London for our wedding.'

'Your wedding?' Emma was delighted. 'When is it? Of course I'll come. I hope you want me to be bridesmaid? Is it to be a formal wedding, or a quiet affair?'

'It's fixed for the last day of October,' Guy said. 'I've got a job in Canada. I have to leave by the fifteenth of November, so this is going to be a pretty tight squeeze, but I couldn't go without Fanny, and she's agreed to do without the usual fuss and trimmings. We're having a quiet little wedding, just family and close friends like you.'

'A white wedding, though,' Fanny said, her chin determined. 'And you most certainly will be my bridesmaid, Em!'

'Yes,' Guy urged. 'Do you think you can manage it? It would ruin everything for Fanny, I think, if you weren't there, Emma.' He smiled at her, his eyes so nice, so full of friendliness, that she was touched. Far from having lost Fanny, she thought, she had gained another friend, even though they were going across to the other side of the world. Distances would not diminish the warmth between them, she was sure of that. It would take more than an air journey to separate her from Fanny.

'I'll manage it somehow,' she promised. 'I'll make my own bridesmaid's dress, something simple. What colour would you like, Fan?'

'Oh, yellow for you, darling,' Fanny said decisively. 'A pretty primrose colour suits you.'

The children were staring, all ears. Emma caught their eyes and laughed. 'I forgot to introduce you ...' She drew them into the circle and told them who Fanny and Guy were, told Fanny and Guy the children's names.

Fanny bent to kiss each one. Tracy was rapt, staring with eyes wide with admiration at Fanny's beautiful golden curls, her delicate heart-shaped face and enormous eyes. 'You're just like the fairy on our Christmas tree!' she burst out.

Emma stifled a smile. Fanny looked startled, then rather shy. But Guy said seriously, 'I know what you mean, Tracy. I feel like that, too,' and the way in which he looked at Fanny made Emma feel very much in the way.

It must be wonderful, she thought wistfully, to have a man look at you like that, as if he saw rainbows and heard trumpets at the very sight of you! She knew the feeling ... every time she saw Ross unexpectedly her heart felt as if it was going through a giant wringer, being crushed in some ruthless machine.

'Come and see our cottage,' Tracy urged, holding Fanny's hand with eager devotion and dragging her towards the door.

'It looks enchanting,' Fanny breathed, gazing at it.

'Yes, go ahead,' Emma nodded. 'I'll put away our gardening tools and join you in a moment. We can have tea. There are plenty of cakes and scones, all home-made and delicious, I can promise you!'

'Edie spent all morning baking,' Tracy confided as she pulled Fanny away.

'Oh, yes, I heard about Edie,' said Fanny, smiling at Emma over her shoulder as she went.

'How did you?' Tracy demanded.

'Emma wrote to me about you all,' Fanny told her.

'Did she?' Tracy was surprised. 'What did she say about me in her letter? Did she say how good I was at cooking?'

Fanny tactfully assured her that Emma had praised her cooking to the skies. Remembering that she had described with gusto the morning when Tracy made concrete porridge, Emma was grateful for Fanny's tact and warm-heartedness.

Robin and Donna, abandoning their gardening without a backward glance, followed into the cottage. Fanny apparently had the same charms for them as she did for Tracy. A new, enchanting face was a big draw when one spent such a quiet life. The children loved to meet new people, talk to visitors.

Guy watched them, smiling. Emma looked up at him, remembering things she had, astonishingly, forgotten about him—that little bump in his nose which he had acquired during a rugger game; the smile in his blue eyes, his curly fair hair and firm chin. Once these things had made her feel weak at the knees. Now she was puzzled. Why had she ever thought she loved him? He was nice, indeed he was charming, but he lacked Ross's strength, the toughness of mind which made Ross such a force to be reckoned with.

Guy turned and looked down at her. 'You look very well yourself,' he said, surveying her.

She laughed. She was wearing old muddy jeans, wellington boots and a thick sweater, which she kept especially for gardening since it had shrunk slightly in the washing process and was no longer exactly high fashion. 'I look a mess! If I'd known you were coming...'

'We wanted to surprise you. Fanny had a few

160

days free, so we thought we'd take a quick trip down here, see you and enjoy some country air at the same time.'

'Where are you staying?' she asked, leaning on her fork.

'Dorchester. Attractive little town, isn't it?'

'You must visit Hardy's birthplace,' she told him.

'We did—on the way here,' he smiled. 'Briefly! Fanny isn't one for prolonged sightseeing.'

Emma laughed, 'Don't I know it! Fanny's favourite occupation has always been sitting in front of a television eating toffees. We were always opposites in that respect. I like to get involved. Fanny likes to watch.'

'She comes to watch me playing rugger every Saturday,' Guy told her grinning. 'She looks like a teddy bear, wrapped up in about fifty thick woolly scarves, with a knitted bobble hat on top of her head and big furry boots . . .' He looked proud. 'The team have adopted her as a mascot. They'll miss her when we leave for Canada. They reckon she brings them luck.'

'You certainly had some luck getting Fanny,' Emma told him, smiling. 'She's a wonderful girl. I love her very dearly, and I hope you'll both be happy for ever.'

Guy took her by the shoulders, his face lit up with joy and certainty. 'Don't you worry about Fanny, I'll always do everything I can to keep her as happy as she is now. I know I'm the luckiest man on earth. My father can't stop telling me so. He thinks Fanny is as close to a fairy princess as I'm likely to get! He can't understand why she's marrying me!' He laughed, bending to kiss Emma's cheek. 'Nor can I!'

Emma hugged him. 'She loves you, that's obvious. And I think you're a perfect match, you complement each other beautifully.'

'What a wonderful girl you are, Emma,' Guy burst out, in gratitude, his voice raised joyfully. He kissed her again, on the lips, briefly. 'How can I ever thank you enough for forgiving me? I came between you, yet you're so wonderfully kind and forgiving...'

'It was only what was to be expected,' she pointed out. 'These things happen. I'm glad, really glad ... honestly! It's going to be wonderful.'

'You can say that again,' he breathed emphatically 'From now on everything is going to be fantastic!'

They both laughed, then to bring them back to normal life Emma said gently, 'Why not go in and let the children show you around? I'll be with you all in a minute, when I've disposed of my tools and cleaned myself up a little!'

'Fine,' he said, and wandered off obediently, while Emma turned to gather up her tools. She knocked the mud off them, counted them carefully. She did not want one out to rust, as had happened before when the children left a trowel out.

Turning to go to the garden shed, she found herself facing Ross. He was leaning over the garden gate, a dark look on his face. What was wrong with him? she wondered.

'Hello! You're back early.' She smiled, hoping to drive away the anger from his face.

'Too early, apparently,' he snapped.

She frowned. 'What's that supposed to mean?'

'How long has Romeo been here?' he demanded, coming into the garden and banging the gate behind him so hard that it flew open again.

'Romeo?' For a moment her mind was blank, then she laughed. 'Do you mean Guy?'

'Guy!' He repeated the name with a stinging sarcasm in his voice. 'Who else?'

'The most marvellous thing has happened,' she said eagerly, hoping to make him smile. 'You'll never guess!'

'Let me try,' he drawled unpleasantly. 'All is suddenly sweetness and light between you! What did he say ... you're such a wonderful girl, Emma, so sweet and forgiving ...' He imitated Guy's voice, emphasising it to the point of sickening over-enthusiasm. His face expressed disgust. 'My God! I could have been sick on the spot. How any sane, intelligent human being could listen to such drivel, believe such humbug ...'

'Guy meant it,' she said angrily. 'Just because all men are not the hard-headed, cold-hearted brutes you are ...'

He was very pale now, his eyes tight points of steely light which pierced her, his jaw projecting furiously in rage. 'Go on, say what you've wanted to say for weeks! Do you imagine I don't know your opinion of me?'

Emma stared, shaken, breathless. 'What?'

'I am well aware how you feel about me,' he said icily.

She was now as white as he was, her whole body shaking. He knew? Horror made her wince in disbelief. She couldn't bear it, she could not bear to contemplate the idea that Ross knew she loved him, that it irritated him and made him despise her.

He caught her shoulders and shook her. 'Don't you turn away from me with that face! Look at me!'

She twisted in his grip, struggling to break away, terrified of the probing grey eyes.

'Let me go! You're hurting me...'

'Don't tempt me,' he said nastily. 'You don't know how much I'd like to! A good hard slap might bring you to your senses. I knew you were an idiot, but I didn't realise how big an idiot you were until now.'

'Have you quarrelled with Amanda again?' she demanded, shaken and puzzled by his anger. Surely it could not be directed at her? It must have been aroused by something else, and now he was expending upon her the rage he felt towards someone he dared not attack.

'Amanda!' The snort was almost violent. 'Don't try to sidetrack me.'

'I'm trying to find out what's put you in this nasty mood,' she said patiently.

He looked down at her, brows dark, mouth curling scornfully. 'As if you didn't know!'

Wide-eyed, she shook her head. 'I think you're punishing me because of something Amanda has done, but I tell you now, I will not put up with it. You're not manhandling me every time you feel like it!'

'Aren't I?' His voice was suddenly dangerously soft. His hands closed on her upper arms, pinching the flesh as he bent her slightly backwards. For a flashing second she felt a wave of disbelief, alarm, weakness, as his face came nearer, his eyes narrowed. Then his mouth covered hers, his lips hard and demanding, seeking and seizing an unwilling yet ardent response from her. She couldn't think. She could only feel, and feel a pleasure that was almost entirely pain.

This kiss was not meant for her—it belonged to Amanda. Ross was still punishing her as a substitute for the girl he loved, and the kiss which might, in other happier circumstances, have been a stinging joy was now only humiliation and grief. Yet she could not pretend to herself that she did not enjoy it. Her traitorous body awoke to life under his touch. Her mouth quivered with heat and pleasure.

Taking a stern grip upon herself, she pulled back from the brink of oblivion, and made herself struggle, slapping Ross hard with her open palm as his head drew away.

'Don't ever do that again!' she gasped.

He released her and stepped back, one finger tracing the red mark where she had slapped him. A curious little smile quirked his mouth. 'I wouldn't like to meet you in a dark alley,' he murmured. 'You have muscles I didn't suspect!'

She did not answer. Her heart was still performing a strange somersault.

Ross shoved his hands into his pockets. 'Well,' he said quietly, 'shall we go in and be hospitable towards your friend? Do you want to put him up for the night? He could share my room.'

She smiled politely. 'That's very kind of you, but he and Fanny will be going back to Dorchester.'

Ross stared down at her. 'Fanny?'

'Yes, my flatmate—I told you about her and Guy. Don't you remember? Well, they drove down to tell me that they're getting married and want me to be their bridesmaid.' She smiled again. 'Isn't that marvellous?'

'Marvellous!' he said in a still, quiet voice.

'I shall make my own dress, but even so they haven't given me much time. They're leaving for Canada, you see, as soon as they're married—they only have a few more weeks in this country. Guy's got a job over there.'

'And they've asked you to be bridesmaid?' Ross looked at her sharply. 'You ought to be crying, not babbling enthusiastically. Asking you that is a piece of crass insensitivity!'

She flushed. 'You forget, they don't know ... they must never even suspect ... that I once imagined I was in love with Guy.'

'Imagined?' His voice was wry. 'I saw your face when he was talking to you just now, remember.'

'I was happy to see him and Fanny,' she said defensively. 'I was glad to be sure that what I'd once felt was all gone now. I'm cured of Guy. It was just a brief spell ... nothing real, nothing solid.'

Ross watched her, his features sardonic. 'So? And the kiss? What was that for?'

She looked blank. 'The kiss?'

'I saw him kissing you,' Ross said curtly.

'Oh ...' She remembered now. 'That didn't mean anything ... it was just a brotherly peck.'

Ross gave her a dangerous, narrow-eyed stare. 'Was it, indeed? Well, don't confuse me with him, will you. Brotherly pecks aren't in my line.'

She was confused, pink-cheeked. What did he mean? Her heart thudded.

Then Robin called from the cottage, his voice shrill and excited. 'Uncle Ross, Emma ... aren't you coming in? We're waiting for tea!'

Emma hurried towards him, reluctant yet oddly eager to get away from the tautness of her encounter with Ross. When she w. alone she would take out the memory of those moments and go over it, see what she had thought and felt. For now she wanted to break away, return to the less spine-tingling realities of life with the three children.

Fanny and Guy were in the kitchen, helping Tracy butter bread, laying out cups and saucers, while the kettle cheerfully bubbled its way towards boiling. Emma introduced Ross to them. He shook hands briefly with Guy, assessed him politely yet with a coolness Emma felt must be noticeable to the others. Then he turned and smiled with much more warmth at Fanny. His eyes flickered appreciatively.

'Emma said you were pretty ... she understated it. You're a peaches and cream girl, aren't you?'

Fanny smiled, dimpling. 'Thank you. Emma didn't tell us you were such a flatterer.'

He gave Emma a little sidelong look, a flick of his dark lashes, a sardonic smile. 'Didn't she?'

'No,' Emma said sweetly. 'I couldn't tell them you were prone to flattery because I'd never seen signs of it.' She smiled at Fanny. 'You're bringing out a new side of him.'

'Feminine girls have that effect on men,' Ross said.

'Ouch!' Emma retorted. 'Thanks.'

'Emma's very feminine,' Guy declared, indignant on her behalf, and bristling at Ross's approach to Fanny.

'You obviously haven't come in contact with her left hook,' Ross drawled. 'She could go three rounds with the world heavyweight champion.'

Fanny opened her blue eyes very wide, staring from him to Emma. 'Goodness!'

Very pink, Emma said, 'The kettle is boiling. Excuse me ... Ross, take them through to the sitting-room, will you, while I finish making the tea?'

'I'll help,' said Fanny with determination.

Ross gestured to Guy. 'We'd better make ourselves scarce. You know what women are like in a kitchen!'

Guy obeyed, but with an expression that boded ill for his future relations with Ross. Guy was an easy-going man, but he had been deliberately offended during the last few moments, and he was aware of it.

'What,' asked Fanny, 'is going on? You didn't give me any hint.'

'Hint about what?' returned Emma casually, pretending to be stupid.

'You know perfectly well,' Fanny said affectionately. 'There's an atmosphere between you two that could be cut with a knife.'

'You're wrong,' said Emma. 'There's another girl.' Her voice was brittle. She hoped Fanny would not hear the underlying pain, but Fanny had known her for too long, and in this case was not made blind by her own feelings.

'Oh, Emma,' she murmured sympathetically. 'Poor darling! What rotten luck.'

Emma shrugged. 'Just one of those things...'

'He's very attractive,' sighed Fanny.

'Very,' Emma agreed tightly.

'In a tough sort of way,' Fanny added thoughtfully. 'I'm not sure I like tough men too much.' She gave Emma a little glance of inquiry. 'You're certain about the other girl? Because I was sure I felt something just now ... something between you...'

'Yes,' Emma said bitterly. 'Irritation! We'd just had a knock-down row. Whenever he falls out with his girl-friend he takes it out on me as the nearest available female.'

'What's she like, this other girl?'

'Blonde and deadly,' Emma returned tartly. 'She glitters and has a vicious tongue. I hope they'll be very happy.'

Fanny laughed. 'Oh, darling! You are in a mood!'

'As Ross said, I'm not very feminine!'

'He was talking through his hat. You're the most feminine girl I know. Look how you've mothered those three children! They've been telling me all about it. You've done a wonderful job here. It all depends what you mean by feminine. If you mean someone who swoons at the sight of blood, flutters her eyelashes when a man looks at her and is too weak to carry anything heavier than a cushion ... then that doesn't include you. But there's much more to a womanly woman than that, and most modern men know it!'

'You're biased in my favour,' said Emma. 'But thank you for the vote of confidence!'

They carried the tea through into the sitting-room, and found the two men deep in a gloomy silence. Guy was flicking through the pages of a country magazine. Ross stood by the window, his profile stony.

Fanny gave Emma an alarmed glance. They poured the tea, handed Guy a cup, asked Ross to sit down. 'A sandwich?' Emma asked him, fluttering her lashes sweetly.

Ross gave her a little smile of indulgent amusement which made her seethe. 'Playing games?' he murmured under his breath as he settled down in a chair.

'I thought you liked that approach,' she retorted. 'The sweet, feminine touch ...'

Guy was nibbling at one of Edie's feather-light scones with appreciation. 'Can you make scones, Fanny?' he asked.

She looked smug. 'Of course!'

'We must have them for tea when we're married,' said Guy.

'If you want to, darling,' Fanny agreed.

Ross was watching Emma, his eyes sardonic. 'Touching scene,' he murmured to her, under cover of reaching for a piece of shortcake. 'Your friend isn't just a pretty face, is she? Wifely submission makes for a happy marriage.'

'Balderdash,' Emma said fiercely. 'Why don't you join the rest of us in the twentieth century, Ross?'

The children were upstairs, playing a noisy game of hide and seek. Suddenly they swept down, in a shouting body, and tore into the room.

'We're starving,' Tracy announced. 'Goody ... scones and fairy cakes, biscuits and chocolate cake!'

Robin sat down on the carpet beside Emma. 'Can we have tea in here today?'

'No,' she said firmly. 'You make too many crumbs. Tea in the kitchen for you three. Come on, I'll supervise.' She detached Donna's tiny fingers from a biscuit. 'Your tea is already laid in the kitchen, sweetie.'

'Choclit cake ...' Donna moaned.

'Some bread and butter first,' Emma asserted firmly.

She led them out of the room, Donna clinging to her hand, Robin close to her, talking fast, his rosy face uplifted to hers. Fanny watched her go with affectionate eyes, and began to dream about a dim and golden future in which she herself would have children clinging to her hands ...

Five minutes later Amanda appeared at the back door, slender and well-groomed in silver-grey, her hair so immaculate that Emma wondered if she carried her own personal atmosphere around with her in order to be impervious to wind and weather. She stood there, casting a distasteful glance over the children as they ate their tea. 'Ross here?' she inquired in a cold drawl.

'In the sitting-room,' Emma nodded.

Amanda drifted past. Emma followed her to ask if she would have a cup of tea. Fanny was talking to Ross, laughing—she looked round as they appeared, and her blue eyes widened. Clearly, she recognised Amanda from the description Emma had given, for she then looked quickly at Ross, who was rising to greet the new arrival.

'Can you come to Queen's Daumaury at once?' Amanda asked him abruptly, ignoring the others. 'I tried to ring, but your telephone was out of order.'

'Is it? I didn't know.' Ross sounded abstracted. 'Look, is it really necessary for me to ... I'm in no mood for another of those scenes.'

'Your father has had a stroke,' said Amanda.

Emma had been watching Ross. She saw the colour leave his skin, his jaw clench. 'Is it serious? Is the doctor there?'

'The doctor got there within ten minutes. We put your father back to bed.' She looked at Ross sombrely. 'I think it's serious this time, Ross. Judith ought to be here. Could she leave hospital? Should I send a car for her?'

Suddenly Emma knew. She saw in a painful flash

172

all that had been dark before. Leon Daumaury was not the father of Judith's husband—he was Judith's father. Ross's father.

Ross would be the next owner of Queen's Daumaury.

CHAPTER TEN

So many things which had puzzled her now fell into place. Ross, as heir to Queen's Daumaury, must have been considered quite a catch by ambitious young women, and his story about the girl who pursued him and tried to blackmail him into marriage now made even more sense—with such a rich prize at stake no wonder the girl had been desperate enough to try any method, however wild and wickedly unscrupulous.

Emma could imagine Ross, hurt and angry, when his father refused to believe his version of events storming out of the house and staying away. Yet he must care deeply about his father, or he would not have stayed so close at hand here in the village. He could have gone anywhere. His profession made him a free man. He could have got work in any part of the world. He had preferred to stay, and that said a great deal for how he really felt about Queen's Daumaury and about his father.

And Leon Daumaury was not as coldly set against Ross as he had appeared whenever she saw them together. He had come here, he had sent for Ross from time to time, and even if they had always quarrelled on these occasions, clearly there was an underlying concern between them, a feeling for each other, which remained despite all the quarrels.

Amanda, too, was more comprehensible. Her unswerving pursuit of Ross, her cryptic hints about him...

No wonder Ross had been evasive, despite his obvious attraction towards Amanda. He probably suspected her motives to be more mercenary than loving, and his other experience of predatory young women must have made him even more determined to steer clear of all such traps.

Ross and Amanda left hurriedly with barely a word, and Emma faced the future with a bleak feeling of emptiness.

Fanny followed her into the kitchen, questions bubbling on her lips, but Emma was not disposed to talk much.

'We must go,' said Guy, seeing how things were.

Fanny opened her mouth to protest, then fell silent, catching his stern eye.

'Shall we see you tomorrow?' she asked Emma. 'We could drive over here.'

'We'll be in the way if there's family trouble,' Guy told her quietly. 'It's a pity, but perhaps we ought to go back to London.'

'No,' Emma said hastily, dragging her mind back to the present with a sigh. 'No, of course you must come over here. Please, do come.'

Fanny kissed her, then kissed the children. Tracy was pale and very quiet. She went with the others to wave goodbye to Guy and Fanny, but Emma noticed that she looked miserable. Bending down, she put an arm around the little girl.

'What's the matter?'

Tracy looked up at her anxiously. 'I heard what Amanda said. Is our grandfather going to die?'

'I hope not, darling,' Emma said gently.

'But he's very old.'

'Yes, but he's strong,' Emma reminded her. 'And he has a very good doctor.' She was sure that a man as rich as Leon Daumaury would have the best doctor that could be found.

The news of his illness actually made its way into the news bulletins that evening. The Daumaury fortune was immense, and share prices began to fall when the news hit the stock market. Any change in the direction of his many companies must make alarming news for shareholders.

Ross did not return that evening. Telephone engineers arrived to work on the telephone, and discovered some trouble with the outside wiring. They rapidly repaired it, and the telephone at once began to ring. Many of Ross's friends were trying to find out the true situation, and Emma grew weary of explaining her own total ignorance.

Mrs Pat popped up during the evening, leaving Edie in charge at the inn, to talk to Emma about the reporters who had descended upon her. They were making the inn their headquarters while it was open.

'It's only a matter of time before one of 'em makes his way up to see you,' Mrs Pat warned her.

'They're like hungry ferrets, they jump at anything. Don't you talk to 'em.'

'I won't,' Emma said grimly. 'What could I tell them? I've never known anything.'

Mrs Pat grimaced, hearing the underlying reproach. 'It wasn't my place to tell what Ross didn't want told, m'dear.'

'I feel such a fool,' Emma sighed.

'Why should you? You've been a tower of strength to Judith in her hour of need.'

'I've been deaf, dumb and blind ever since I got here,' Emma said hotly. 'I took Ross for an ordinary run-of-the-mill vet. Instead of that, he's the son of a multi-millionaire who will inherit an enormous fortune very soon. Ross is about as ordinary as gunpowder.'

'Even gunpowder is ordinary if you work with it long enough,' said Mrs Pat, chuckling with amusement. She gave Emma a shrewd look. 'You sound disappointed to find he's going to be a rich man?'

Emma flushed. 'It's no business of mine,' she said with an evasive look.

'Isn't it?' Mrs Pat smiled.

When she had gone, Emma tidied the cottage with the sort of obsessive attention to detail one gives when one needs to drug one's mind with work. Just as she was about to go to bed, the telephone rang. She answered it warily, remembering what Mrs Pat had said, but it was Ross, not a newspaper reporter.

'How are things down there?' he asked abruptly.

'Fine,' she said. 'How is your father?'

'Holding his own,' he said in a comparatively cheerful tone. 'Judith is here, and wants to come down to you for the night, since it looks as if there isn't going to be any sort of emergency here after all. Would it be convenient?'

'Of course it would. This is your house, not mine,' Emma told him.

'Judith can have my room,' said Ross. He paused. 'Are you sure things are all right? You sound a bit uptight.'

'I'm tense, I suppose,' she said. 'I was concerned about your father.'

There was another silence. 'Angry with me for not telling you?' he asked her shrewdly.

'It was none of my business,' she said.

'I can tell that you are,' he said. 'I'm sorry, but I had my reasons.'

'I'm aware of that. You told me at the beginning —if I'd known who you were I might have chased after you like all the other girls you've ever known.' Because of her own hurt she spoke with stinging mockery, hoping to make him angry, as if his anger might ease her own pain a little.

'It wasn't like that,' he said.

'No?' She was icily incredulous.

'Not the way you put it,' he said, beginning now to get angry. 'You're putting a totally false construction on it.'

'It doesn't matter,' she said, wanting to end the conversation. 'Really, it's a matter of indifference to me whether you told me or not.'

'I see,' said Ross. 'Well, goodnight, then.'

She heard the crash of the receiver at his end and stared at the telephone dumbly. He had hung up.

The sleek Daumaury limousine delivered Judith at the cottage half an hour later. Emma heard the car purring down the lane, and met her at the gate.

Judith kissed her on the cheek with almost sisterly warmth. 'Oh, it's so good to see you, so good to be here!'

'You look tired,' Emma said with concern. 'Have you eaten?'

Judith smiled. 'More than enough! You've no idea what it was like at the house ... the servants have nothing else to do but make meals and serve them, and they kept trotting out food all evening, as if only by feeding us could they stop themselves sinking into melancholy. They're fond of the old man, you know.'

Emma smiled, believing it to be very easy to become fond of Leon Daumaury. He had such a tired, desolate air at times. All his money could not armour him against personal loneliness.

Judith sank into a chair in front of the banked fire, stretching out her stockinged toes to the flames, her shoes kicked off casually into a corner.

'I'm dead beat! They whisked me out of hospital with the news, and I sat for the whole journey expecting the worst, only to find, when I finally got to him, that Father was already beginning to fight back. It will take more than a slight stroke to finish him!' Her face and voice expressed a shy pride. 'He's a tough old fellow, you know.'

'Toughness seems to be a family characteristic,' Emma said, thinking of Ross.

Judith stared, puzzled, then grinned. 'Oh, you're talking about my dear brother?'

'He has a hide like leather and a mind like the edge of a knife,' Emma said bitterly.

Judith gazed at her, wide-eyed. 'Oh ...' For a few seconds she was quiet, her lips parted in surprised thought. Then she smiled warmly. 'I like you, Emma. By the way, Father likes you, too—he told me so tonight. He told Ross that if he married you he would cut him off without a farthing.'

Emma went scarlet, then white, her breath knocked out of her. Then she said weakly, 'Why on earth should he imagine that Ross and I ... whatever did Ross say?'

'He said that since farthings were no longer legal tender he didn't give a hoot. If he wanted to marry you he would, and Father could put all his unwanted farthings into the poor box.'

Emma knotted her trembling fingers together. 'But there's no question of ... I mean, Ross was joking. We're not ... there's nothing between Ross and me.'

Judith peeped at her from between thick lashes. 'No? I didn't get that impression. The nurse was most upset about it all, but Father looked quite elated. He always enjoys a good squabble with Ross. It's the breath of life to him. Amanda, though ...' Judith giggled. 'Amanda looked pretty sick about it all.'

'Amanda heard all this?' Emma was aghast. 'But,

180

Judith, it's Amanda Ross loves, it's Amanda he'll marry...'

Judith yawned. 'Dear Emma, I must buy you a white stick and a guide dog. You're the blindest girl I've ever met.' She rose. 'I'm off to bed. Goodnight.'

Emma stared after her, confused and incredulous. What on earth did she mean?

She bent and attended to the fire, shovelling ash over the flames to make sure that they would not entirely consume the coal during the night, keeping the room warm so that in the morning they would get up and find the temperature comfortable. It was already beginning to be chilly in the early morning. Autumn would be upon them soon.

Then she went upstairs to bed, feeling depressed and weary. She was just getting in between the sheets when she heard a sound downstairs which alarmed her. Someone was moving about down there!

She tiptoed out and crept down the stairs. A light showed beneath the kitchen door. She got the poker from the sitting-room and crept slowly up to the kitchen door, paused, taking a deep breath, then flung it open and burst into the room, poker raised ready for use.

Ross was at the stove, frying himself an egg. He swung round, stared and burst out laughing.

'What's this? The Charge of the Light Brigade?'

Furiously she said, 'I thought you were a burglar! You're lucky I didn't break your head open with this!'

'I believe you,' he said mockingly. 'I know how

you lay about you when roused, remember? What a terrifying girl you are! Fists one minute, pokers the next ... I hate to think what married life will be like with a virago like you!'

She opened her eyes wide, flushing. 'That's never likely to concern you, so you needn't worry about it.'

'Oh, but it does,' he said, returning cheerfully to his cooking, his back towards her so that she could no longer see the expression on his face.

She bit her lip. Was he teasing her? 'It does?' she asked in faltering tones.

'I intend to marry you,' he said in a voice so casual that for a full moment she thought her ears were playing tricks.

Then her temper flared at the maddening self-confidence that could give birth to such a statement. 'Oh, you do?' Her voice quivered with rage. 'I presume that my opinions and wishes have nothing to do with the matter? You've decided to marry me, and that's that? Well, let me tell you something—I wouldn't marry you if you were the last man in the world! I know why you've decided to marry me, you know!'

He finished his cooking, served the food on to a warm plate and slid it into the oven to keep warm. Then he turned and surveyed her, eyes mocking.

'So why do I want to marry you?'

'To irritate your father!'

He laughed out loud.

Furiously, she burst out, 'Judith told me about the row you had with him! It had never entered your head to marry me until he said he wouldn't permit it. Then, with typical obstinacy, you made up your mind to go ahead and do just that, to annoy him.'

Ross caught her shoulders and pulled her close, his eyes smiling into hers. 'Silly girl! The notions you get! What sane man would behave like that? My father doesn't fool me. He wants me to marry you, that's why he warned me off ... I'd already hinted at the possibility, and in his cussed fashion he was delighted, but he would hate me to know that, so he pretended to be annoyed. He knew I'd do just what I wanted to in the end. He likes you— I could tell by the way he spoke of you.'

'I must be going out of my mind,' she said dazedly. 'You talk about marriage as if it were an inevitable fact, yet you know very well that you and I are a million miles apart. We've never been on marriage terms...'

'We kissed, didn't we?' His eyes challenged her to remember it. 'Why, we even shared a bike! How much closer can you get?'

'Oh, don't be absurd,' she snapped. 'You kissed me to work out a fit of temper.'

'I kissed you because I'd been wanting to do just that for days,' he said tightly. 'And I want to do it again. Now.'

She instinctively moved back, but his hands were too strong, holding her firmly as he bent his head. His kiss this time was gentler, but just as compelling, drawing her emotions upwards until she shook with answering passion, her arms sliding round his neck to touch the hair at the back of his head.

When he drew back a little they were both shaken. Ross smiled down at her. 'Will you marry me, Emma?'

'Ross,' she whispered, putting her face against his chest to hide the burning heat of her cheeks for a moment. 'What about Amanda, Ross?'

He laughed. She felt the quiver of it in his chest muscles. 'Oh, Amanda ...' he murmured. 'You can't seriously have believed I would fall for Amanda's corny old line? I've known her for years, remember. She's a distant cousin, a poor relation who came to live with us when her family broke up. I know her —only too well! She's always been an opportunist; unscrupulous, malicious, ambitious and a lot of other unpleasant things! My father kept her around because she was a decorative hostess. He paid dearly for the service. She charged everything—clothes, jewels, anything that took her fancy.'

'You always seemed amused by her ...'

'She can be an amusing companion,' he admitted. 'She's easy to look at, after all.'

'You did find her attractive, then,' she flared.

'Jealous?' Ross was amused, his eyes mocking her as he grinned at her.

'You must have been drawn to her once,' she said with pain. 'I sensed it, an intimacy between you.'

'I've known her for years,' he said, shrugging. 'She was a beautiful cannibal, all teeth and claws— I was wary of her, but at the same time I was able to admire her beauty.'

'She certainly expected to marry you!'

Ross looked stern, brows a dark line. 'I never encouraged such hopes—far from it! You mustn't be sentimental about her, Emma. She felt nothing for me; you know—it was all pretence, and I knew it. She's an ambitious girl, Amanda. I doubt if she's capable of a genuine emotion.'

'I wonder if you are either,' Emma said, the words wrung from her out of her pain and uncertainty. He had kissed her, he had asked her to marry him. But those three little words had not passed his lips.

'What?' He stared at her, going pale. 'What is it? Emma, I thought...'

'You thought that the wonderful, irresistible Ross Daumaury only had to snap a finger for any girl to fall swooning at his feet, I suppose?' She looked at him scathingly. 'Well, you were wrong.'

He caught her close, his arms an unbending prison as she struggled to break free. 'What are you talking about, you halfwit?'

'You're altogether too sure of yourself,' she said bitterly, relinquishing the attempt to get away. 'Just because you think yourself irresistible ... saying you knew how I felt!' She snorted scornfully. 'You know nothing of the kind!'

His face cleared. 'You're talking about what I said this morning? But I thought you were going back to Guy, then. I was furious. I wanted to wring your neck. When I said that I knew how you felt about me, I meant that I thought you detested me. I thought I had no chance at all ...'

'But now?' she asked.

'After I'd kissed you this morning, I felt much

more hopeful,' he admitted. 'I knew you weren't going back to Guy, by then, and your response had been pretty terrific. I began to have high hopes again. Then Amanda said something ...'

'I can imagine,' said Emma drily.

'Yes, she was her usual charming self—said you were in the throes of a schoolgirl crush on me, nothing more! She meant to be beastly, but it made me feel marvellous!'

'Oh, did it?' Emma asked him sarcastically.

He grinned. 'I'm afraid so!' He lifted her chin with one finger and gazed into her eyes. 'Tell me the truth, darling. Do you love me?'

'I haven't heard you saying those three magic words yet,' she pointed out.

He looked blank. 'What? But you know I love you ... I've said so in twenty different ways already.'

Her heart thudding, she murmured, 'Say it again, just once. I'm a simple-minded soul. I like the old-fashioned words said the old-fashioned way. Just ... I love you ...'

He said the words, in a deep, shaken voice, and she repeated them after him, then flung her arms around his neck.

'Oh, Ross, I do love you so,' she underlined.

For a while there was a silence so thick and dark it was like a starless midnight, then Ross lifted his mouth reluctantly from hers and said abstractedly, 'I must eat my supper. I'm starving.'

'Well, really, Ross!' giggled Emma. 'How very unromantic of you!'

'I haven't eaten since tea time,' he said. 'I

couldn't touch food while I was worried about my father.' He looked at her with anxiety. 'Will you be able to face living at Queen's Daumaury? I know how much you love the simple life.'

She gave a little sigh. 'Must we go there at once? Your father may recover completely. We could stay here then.'

'Eventually we must live there, though,' he said. 'It's a very beautiful house, and I'm rather fond of it. Amanda knows that and she played on my feelings for what they were worth. Her own devotion to the house is skin-deep.'

'I thought it very beautiful,' Emma admitted. 'But rather cold.'

'You would bring it back to life,' he said. 'Queen's Daumaury has lacked a soul ever since my mother died. It needs you. My father needs you, too. Now that he's reconciled to Judith's marriage, the house will always have children in it ... first hers, then ours ...'

'Hold on,' she said, blushing. 'We aren't even married yet!'

'We will be soon,' he said. 'I'm not a patient man. I want you too much to wait for you. I've waited long enough already. I never hoped to find a girl like you—one who genuinely did not care about my money, one who loved me for myself. That was why I tried to stop you finding out who I was. I think I knew I loved you from that first meeting. I was afraid to see your face if you knew about my father. I was afraid things would change between us. But that was only in the beginning. I hadn't known you very long before I became sure that my money would not attract you, in the least. It might put you off, but you would never chase me because of it.'

'It's a big responsibility,' she said gravely. 'I'm afraid I do rather wish you didn't have it. I haven't been brought up to that sort of life. I may not be suitable to act as a hostess at Queen's Daumaury. I'm no Amanda, you know.'

'Oh, I know that, my funny darling,' Ross said, laughing. 'That's what I love you for ... your honesty, your directness, your integrity.'

'Oh, and I thought it was for my lovely face,' she said, pretending to be hurt.

He pinched her cheek. 'Don't be pert! There are other things about you ...'

Emma lifted her face for his kiss, clinging passionately. 'Mmmm, that's nice,' she whispered. 'Tell me more ...'

'We've got all our lives to talk,' he said. 'Just now I only want to kiss you.'

An epic novel of exotic rituals
and the lure of the Upper Amazon

THE TAKERS RIVER OF GOLD

JERRY AND S.A. AHERN

THE TAKERS are the intrepid Josh Culhane and the seductive Mary Mulrooney. These two adventurers launch an incredible journey into the Brazilian rain forest. Far upriver, the jungle yields its deepest secret—the lost city of the Amazon warrior women!

THE TAKERS series is making publishing history. Awarded *The Romantic Times* first prize for High Adventure in 1984, the opening book in the series was hailed by *The Romantic Times* as "the next trend in romance writing and reading. Highly recommended!"

Jerry and S.A. Ahern have never been better!

TAK–3

Share the joys and sorrows
of real-life love with
Harlequin American Romance! ᵀ·ᴹ·

GET THIS BOOK
FREE as your introduction to
Harlequin American Romance —
an exciting series of romance
novels written especially for
the American woman of today.

Mail to:
Harlequin Reader Service

In the U.S.	In Canada
2504 West Southern Ave.	P.O. Box 2800, Postal Station A
Tempe, AZ 85282	5170 Yonge St., Willowdale, Ont. M2N 6J3

YES! I want to be one of the first to discover
Harlequin American Romance. Send me FREE and without
obligation *Twice in a Lifetime.* If you do not hear from me after I
have examined my FREE book, please send me the 4 new
Harlequin American Romances each month as soon as they
come off the presses. I understand that I will be billed only $2.25
for each book (total $9.00). There are no shipping or handling
charges. There is no minimum number of books that I have to
purchase. In fact, I may cancel this arrangement at any time.
Twice in a Lifetime is mine to keep as a FREE gift, even if I do not
buy any additional books.   154 BPA NAZJ

Name   (please print)

Address   Apt. no.

City   State/Prov.   Zip/Postal Code

Signature (If under 18, parent or guardian must sign.)

AMR-SUB-1

This offer is limited to one order per household and not valid to current Harlequin
American Romance subscribers. We reserve the right to exercise discretion in
granting membership. If price changes are necessary, you will be notified.